THE WARSAW BALLROOM

Soundtrack at the Spotify Playlist: *The Warsaw Ballroom*

Second Edition by Kindle Direct Publishing
An Amazon Company
7290 Investment Drive, Unit B
North Charleston, SC 29418

ISBN-13: 978-1722125943
ISBN-10: 1722125942

10 9 8 7 6 5 4 3 2

Cover by CreateSpace/William Welch

This book is a work of fiction. The characters and incidents are products of the writer's imagination or have been used fictitiously and are not to be construed as real. However, many of the locales in the novel are real and an important part of the characters' histories.

This book is dedicated to friends on a small Cape Cod island, some with four legs.

Hush-a-by lady, in Alice's lap!
Till the feast's ready, we've time for a nap:
When the feast's over, we'll go to the ball —
Red Queen, and White Queen, and Alice, and all!

Lewis Carroll

THE ANNIVERSARY PARTY

The beach between 12th and 13th was the place to be seen after a morning at Jeremiah's Gym. Michael preferred a bike ride to Books & Books on Lincoln Road and later, a swim in the warm, aquamarine water at sunset. Anthony preferred to socialize on the hot, white sand in the midday sun. The beach provided time for contemplation and solitude as well as a place for petty gossip and community. Some of their beachgoer friends, in the line of adjacent towels, remembered the first anniversary. They were the most animated about the second.

Michael woke from a much needed nap to the familiar smells of garlic, onion, and tomatoes from Anthony's simmering sauce. Pasta was perfect before a night of hard partying, and probably the last good meal for a day. Carlos came over for dinner already dressed in his club attire. He had dyed his jeans yellow that morning. His black sleeveless tee was wet from the walk, so he was happy to get into the air conditioned apartment. Anthony's pasta dinner reminded Michael of Boston. Everything else in South Beach was different, especially the clothes and accessories in his closet.

"I'll do the dishes. You two go get ready," Carlos told them. Cutoff jeans and boots were the look if you had the legs. Anthony did, Michael didn't. Jeans, Doc Martins and a dog tag worked.

Leaving the apartment, they got hit with a wall of humidity. That climate contrast still sometimes surprised Michael. As they walked the few blocks to Washington for coffee, the Beach transition had paused for the night. Michael thought there was nothing more beautiful than a newly restored Art Deco building. He was living in Miami's Art Deco District, a neighborhood which is home to the country's largest concentrated collection of Art Deco and recognized by the National Register of Historic Places.

The usual daily morning ritual for Cuban-Americans in this Art Deco playground became Michael's pre-Warsaw jolt. A thimble-sized paper cup of Café Cubano was shot at the Washington Avenue ventanita every Wednesday and Saturday night. The line of weather-worn and heavily made-up faces was not there to savor the sweet richness, but to feed the energy needed for the evening to come.

So, in a proper espresso machine, four scoops of sugar are placed in the brewing carafe. As the espresso flows into the carafe, the brewer stops and stirs the mix into a paste. When the brewing finishes, the espumita layer of pure adrenaline forms. "Una colada, por favor." Carlos orders the several ounces of coffee in a Styrofoam cup to be shared. He pours into the thimble cups and the friends shoot their cafecitos. Each time, Michael remembers the buchi from Boca Chica. "Okay, vamos!" as the three head toward Collins.

Michael never understood why they didn't have to wait in the club line at the corner of Collins and Española Way. That just wasn't something Carlos and Anthony ever needed to do. The South Beach daily rhythm wouldn't call for that. Anthony had adapted to that SoBe rhythm easily. Although Michael was early on the curve, Anthony always made sure he was still on it. Their preparation for the evening began at the beach and ended with a knowing nod from Jaime as he raised the red velvet rope.

Built in 1939 by Jack Hohauser, the Warsaw Ballroom had passed through numerous replications from a cafeteria to Club Ovo, China Club and the Rhythm Club. A streamlined, nautical Art Deco beauty with glass brick, curved edges, and neon lighting, by 1989, Warsaw had become the required SoBe experience of house and ecstasy induced debauchery. George and Leo Nunez were the current owners of this pulsing, tribal-techno-electronic, laser-lit club. They never failed to give the sweet, sweat-smelling sea of bodies the unexpected escape that made the waiting in line worth it. Everyone anticipated a brilliant re-design for the second anniversary, but George Tamsitt had out-done himself.

Jacqueline made sure everyone paid tonight. She was renowned from Boston to Ogunquit, Key West to South Beach, always working with her orange tabby, blond bouffant, and bejeweled fingers. Michael and Jacqueline knew each other from Key West Copa days. "Hello Michael," she winked at him. "Ten dollars boys." Michael reaches in, kisses Jacqueline on her hand, and pats the cat.

The three friends worked their way through the familiar path toward their spot at the oblong bar. Once in a while this parcel would be ignorantly occupied. Dominant males always have their way of marking and taking territory. Again, Michael was impressed at how smoothly the conquest occurred. He looked around the club in awe. Anthony took advantage of his open mouth and carefully put the bitter tasting, white pill on his tongue.

"Close your mouth, babe," Anthony whispered with that dimpled smile that he saved for trusted friends and Cuban muscle boys. Without asking, the bartender placed three ice-cold bottles of water on the bar in front of them and quickly moved to take an order from the other side. Michael placed three singles near the puddle of condensation as the bartender glanced over with a sensual wink.

Crown Royal on the rocks was Michael's drink of choice. Water would be the drink of necessity tonight. They were out earlier than usual because the Anniversary Party was a choreographed event.

Beginning with that swig of water to relieve the bitterness lingering on the tongue, and ending with the after-hour's sunrise, he anticipated a night of ecstasy enhanced sensory overload.

Michael looked around the club. The sight of all the celebratory props amused and baffled, in preparation for a rumored floorshow of "fat ladies, midgets, and pigs." A ten-foot, gigantic, gold-colored, fiberglass penis at the other end of the bar towered over the newly tanned size-queens gathering around it. "There's a stepladder for the penis!" he announced, interrupting Anthony's dimpled attention toward the bartender.

Michael felt the volume of the music suddenly intensify. Deep tribal base reverberated through his core. Taking control, like the conductor of a symphony, was internationally renowned resident DJ, David Padilla. He also felt that all too familiar queasiness, always fleeting, soon to be followed by waves of sweat and warm rush, transitioning into pure bliss and jaw clenching.

Martha Walsh commands everybody a cappella, dance! The house lights go black. In total blackness, she repeats the order, dance now! Padilla choreographs the dramatic pause in total silence and darkness. Cutting through the sight and sound void of the Looking-glass House, Freedom Williams answers in a tribal rap to keep dancing! Taking advantage of the darkness, the Art of Seduction dancers appear, waiting on platforms around the floor. In a burst of intense white light, the music unfolds the beginning of a five-hour human bonding, with go-go boys and drag queens assisting in the conducting of the performances.

In the new light, each perfectly sculpted body knew how to seduce from their platforms. Experience on the circus trapeze and football field prepared the go-go boys for the athletic marathon. The Art of Seduction dancers were the best in South Florida. They respected their Spanish-Romani boss, as he demanded professionalism and athleticism. There was no tolerance for anything that would diminish the reputation he had developed over the years.

The tops of the speakers belonged to the drag queens. The competition to be the most outrageously fabulous was illustrious. After some shopping at Merle's Closet and a few hours of primping, the girls were ready for their performances. Wanda appeared covered in tampons. A bald Kitty Meow undulated in a three-foot headdress. Daisy Deadpetals strutted in red platform pumps. Connie Casserole sashayed with her updo adorned in silk butterflies.

Michael felt his arm as it began to sweat. As he continued to caress himself, he asks Anthony "Are you feeling anything?"

"Not yet, but I always take a little longer than you," he said, looking behind Michael. Swaying to the beat, he grabbed Michael, turned him and

10

pulled him in close, running his hands up and down his belly. "Fuck, will you look at that!"

Michael focused toward the end of the bar. An enormous woman was being escorted through the crowd to the stepladder. With a go-go muscle boy at each arm, she was supported at each ascending step. Assuming this had been rehearsed, Michael watched in amazement as the two men gracefully jumped and perched themselves on top of the bar counter. Now, instead of lifting, they were pulling. The purpose of the penis became evident at that moment. As one guy held the shaft in place, the other assisted the four hundred pounds into position onto the balls. Looking relieved, the boys jumped off the counter and returned to their platforms. The woman arranged the pinafore worn over her knee-length, puffed-sleeve dress and forced an exhausted smile.

Michael continued to watch, as a two-foot Batman was lifted up onto the bar. Boston Red Sox fans would someday know him as "Pedro's midget good-luck charm". They knew him as the guy in the Guinness Book of Records that danced at their knees. Tonight, as part of the show, he crawled onto Alice's obese lap and whispered "Let's follow the White Rabbit," and gave her a kiss on the cheek.

Madonna then began to chant in a trip hop, beat heavy, breathless voice of want and need. The green laser fan moved over the dancefloor to the minimalist house beat. David loves the music he plays, personal and risky. His technique is sublime, carefully planned to support the crowd's ebb and flow. They trust he will work them hard, followed by some time to recover.

Michael thought it was still early, but maybe not, as XTC affects perception of time, its dilation. Sometimes five minutes feels like hours, other times an hour passes by in minutes. The shows usually began hours into the evening, but this was the Anniversary Party. The raised catwalk high above the dance floor extended the stage shows around the perimeter. Silhouetted ballet dancers sensually flowed from the stage to take their places on the metal walkway. The black, faceless, intersex couples gyrated to the *Justify* drum loop mix and synthesized notes.

Anthony and Carlos, returning from the dance floor, hand their wet T-shirts to the bartender. "Up for a walk around?" Anthony asked Michael.

Traveling around the club would get more difficult as the line trickled in through the raised rope. Anthony had no patience and would take Michael by the hand and shove his way through any unfamiliar group. They looked up at the occupied penis, waved to Jacqueline, passed by two work-booted dancers, and followed the catwalk past the stage, to the VIP stairs. Security was working the bottom of the stairs to the VIP area, proof that Warsaw was the place to be seen.

Those stairs provided some level of privacy and pampering. Madonna, Versace, Stallone, Bernhard, Allen, Cruz, Gaultier, Boy George, KC, Marky Mark and Estefan used that trusted, guarded space to overlook the tribal debauchery. Security whispered something to Anthony and small packets were transferred.

The three returned to their corner of the bar. Anthony looked over at the penis and questioned Michael. "Didn't we see her singing in Provincetown?"

"I think that's The Bear?" shocked, remembering fun times on the catamaran. "Damn!"

Michael knew he would need a Crown on the rocks to leave the comfort of that corner. He also knew mixing might cloud the evening. The bartender held up another water and he shook his head. A minute later, the smooth, easy drinking whiskey was in front of him. Sips started with just a little bite of lemon sherried sweetness, followed by a long finish of spice and oak. All the senses were in overdrive now.

Michael wasn't really ready to dance yet, but he would dance to any Franky Knuckles mix. David tempted the crowd with a little bit of that flute double trill, and he knew what was coming. "Come on," Anthony took Michael by the hand. The three friends centered themselves under the green laser fan and let the musical notes come to life. Michael closed his eyes and *The Whistle Song* brought him into another state of mind, a feeling of complete induced euphoria. The music was getting into him and the dancefloor became the communal experience unique to Warsaw.

Michael had been doing XTC for a few years, but he only needed and wanted one hit tonight. Anthony required more. They returned to the bar and their bottles of water. Dancing with a bar break would replay for the rest of the night. They were settling in for the duration.

As Anthony washed down pill number two, Michael needed to stay close to his friend, feeling hot and cold from the sweat. "It's OK if you want to hold me," Anthony tells him. Accepting the offer allowed both to explore each other's bodies with a lack of inhibition. Michael rests his cheek on the sweaty, muscular wing of Anthony's back. The smooth, Italian skin was amazing to the touch. As Carlos joined them, David's music surged through the hundreds with a tribal rhythm and intimacy.

Some time passed. Knowing he could always return to the tethered safeness of their corner, Michael decided to roam. Curious about a different perspective of the penis performance, he stopped at the other end of the bar. The Batman mask made that nose seem huge. What exactly was Michael seeing? Was it extreme performance art, theater of the absurd, or simply a Barnum curiosity? It was certainly two people on opposite

14

sides of a spectrum, performing just like everyone else. Although the awkward dance moves on The Bear's lap made Michael wonder if he was listening to different music, he certainly was enjoying himself. Michael wasn't sure about The Bear.

David was beginning one of his marathon sets. This pioneer was about to give his international following an experience in early progressive house trance. Michael understood why he was starting to be called The Machine. This mix was purely instrumental and Michael was about to join the gradual build-up and dance through the climax. He remembered Anthony once told him dancing to a Padilla mix was like becoming an African tribal dancer. He unbuttoned his black, sweat soaked sleeveless shirt, looped it onto his belt, and let the four-on-the-floor move his feet.

The energy was hypnotic, from a place unfamiliar. Familiar was the Saint, Metro, 1270, Tunnel, Woody's, and Copa. This was anomalous. This was Warsaw. Raw, uninhibited, and euphoric. Michael glanced over at the unoccupied penis as his wondering was relieved. Down at his knees was Batman. Always carried to and from the dance floor, surrounded by his friends for protection, he was moving as if still on The Bear's lap. With a kick drum at every heartbeat, the little man certainly danced to a different drummer.

Floods hit the stage, as Cher interrupted the trance, promising to give the crowd the stars flickering above the dancefloor. Michael didn't mind being interrupted by that contralto voice. The Art of Seduction dancers, dressed as sailors, escorted the drag Cher as she sang about turning back time. Strutting across the stage in her black stiletto heels, her fishnet black stocking and black assless onesie, she successfully pulled off the illusion.

Another marathon set is launched. As the go-go dancers and drag queens take their places, the dancefloor is ready for whatever The Machine will do to them. A repetitive four-on-the-floor with crisp open high hat cymbals accompany the piano in the same rhythm, and base feathering unifies the movement. The rhythm of a fetal heart rate, the beat used by South American shamans, the music and lighting all fine-tuned to elicit altered states of consciousness. Michael spots Anthony and Carlos and dances over to them. Their brains loaded with serotonin and dopamine, the three friends experience an intense feeling of empathy and closeness with each other, the Warsaw revelers, and DJ Padilla.

David utilizes the African dance concept of polyrhythm. While the dancer's shoulders, chest, pelvis, arms and legs move with different rhythms as a total body articulation, there is a main beat. The African cross-beats are life's challenges, while the main beat keeps the community grounded. In many of those communities there aren't the words for rhythm or even music. Rhythm is life itself. Music is the interdependence of human relationships. Skilled dancers blend distinct rhythms independent of those in the music. The celebration of survival.

He sends his Goa Flamenco trance mix out to the Art of Seduction dancers on the stage. *Mescalito* would push the endurance limits of the floor and induce the trance as if from the flowering heads of the peyote used in Native American tribal ceremonies. The principal active component, mescaline, produced those feelings of ecstasy, as the lead dancer closed his eyes and let the music take him to the flamencos of Andalucía.

Michael is on the cusp of moving from the main beat to the cross-beats, to an altered state of consciousness and time. Yet, he is aware of the celebration around him. The performers' rhythm and Anthony and Carlos ground him. He begins to feel the interdependence of this moment in time.

Through that altered state, the drag queens interchanged the ballet dancers up on the catwalk. Stealthily, gracefully, the go-go boys are horizontally passed along the erotic conveyor belt, with their backs to the dance floor. The physical strength needed to pull off this pseudo-fellacio was impressive. Jacqueline worried that the Miami Beach police might not be as impressed with this latest transgression. But the sea of bodies just got the unexpected escape that they waited in line for and the exaggerated beach stories would become legend.

Time passes and the E7 arpeggio chord is rolled up the piano in different inversions and back down again. Everyone knows the celebration is almost over. This is David's signature last song. The flood hits The Bear, and in one of the most beautiful voices Warsaw has ever heard, she sings Gloria Gaynor's *I Will Survive*, that message of personal strength and defiance, from which fear turns into a resolution of survival, and love.

The house lights come on to a round of applause, followed by security forcefully suggesting that everyone finish their drinks and head toward the door. But everyone isn't done. After-hours begins now. The crowd hangs outside while old and new friends decide how they will spend the early morning. "Come with us Michael. Let's close the Deuce," Carlos announces as they head to 14th Street.

Opened just after prohibition in 1926, Mac's Club Deuce is a dingy, stale beer smelling definition of a dive bar. Carlos knows the owner, of course. Mac has owned the bar since 1963 and has worked in his signature Hawaiian shirt every day since. The large neon clock in the window shows 4:15. Michael wanted to swim at sunrise but they were on the bayside of the Beach now. He would have another Crown instead. Loud, dark and smoky, Michael thought he saw Keith Richards and Mickey

Rourke. They head over to the wave shaped bar and order their whiskeys.

"Three?" Mac got the nod from Carlos and began pouring. "You boys have fun tonight?"

"It was insanely fun," Carlos answered. Others standing around, assuming the insanity was Warsaw, agreed.

As they walked home, sunrise brought to life the palette of tropical pinks, lemons, and blues. In his *Pastel Paradise*, Leonard Horowitz looked at the sun, the sky, the seas and the beach and pulled out these colors and painted them on each building. Michael was grateful for Leonard's eccentricity. He felt the sun, sky, seas, and beach on his skin, and thought back at the night, as Cher's voice earwormed into his head.

This cast of characters, brought together to celebrate the two-year existence of this bohemian place, at this particular time in Michael's life, simply made him smile. His body collapsed onto his bed, and as his mind started to slowly blur, he wondered what life events convoked this nexus?

MICHAEL

Boston's First Night festivities and fireworks had been over for hours. Michael and Andy were walking down Mass Ave to their new apartment in the South End. After welcoming in the new year at the 1270 and too drunk to realize the threat behind them, three men quickly descended the brownstone stairs. A gay ghetto in transition, newcomers were often on the receiving end of gentrification anger. Seconds after the metal pipe connected with a stunning thud to his head, the anger transferred to Michael. They chased the attackers for a block before Andy stopped him. "Welcome to Boston," he said as he reached out to check the side of Michael's head. "Let's get you home, call the police, and put some ice on that."

The following week, Michael's car was stolen. Key West seemed like the perfect respite. Never having had a frost, it was time to escape the Boston cold. Hanging at one of the four pools at Simonton Court had become their regular vacation oasis. Blue Heaven for breakfast, with its roaming chickens and sunbathing cats. Sometimes they would get out on the water on a clothing optional sail to the reef. Sometimes lunch at the Pier House.

Applauding the sun as it sets at Mallory Dock allegedly began with Tennessee Williams. Michael always looked forward to a warm chocolate chip cookie from the Cookie Lady as she rode the Square on her bike. As one of the founders of the Key West Cultural Preservation Society, the organization managed Sunset and ensured its artistic integrity. The pre-twilight celebration of magicians, jugglers, clowns, musicians, artists, and food vendors joins locals and visitors from around the world. Watching Dominique and his Flying House Cats sashay on the miniature high-wire is one of the many ritual sunset experiences. At the moment the sun sinks into the Gulf of Mexico, the bagpipes go quiet so that the audience can hear the sizzle, and show their appreciation in applause. Then off to low tea at La Te Da, followed by dinner at Antonia's.

A few doors down from the restaurant was the Copa. A converted movie theater, Jacqueline welcomed club goers from the ticket booth. Michael had heard she was from Boston. He liked her from the start. "Hello dears," she said, sounding more like a Southerner.

"Hi," in unison, "We're from the South End of Boston," said Michael. "Aren't you from Boston, too?"

"I am. That was many years ago, honey," she answered. "South Boston, very different than the South End." Everyone nodding their heads in agreement. "I'm Jacqueline," as she offered her hand to kiss. "Where you boys staying?"

"Simonton Court. We love it there," Andy looked at Michael. "We come down as often as possible."

"Ah yes, Steve and Cameron's place. Have they booked a schooner sail for you yet?"

"Yeah, we went out to the reef yesterday. Gorgeous. The coral was nice, too," Michael said. Everyone knew who he was talking about.

"You two should come to Boca Chica for sunrise. See me at closing."

The taxi van was waiting in front of the club on Duval. "Boca Chica Lounge?" the driver asked, as he opened the passenger side door for Jacqueline. The Copa employees were off for the night and it was time to party. Michael was thinking they'd be home and in bed by now in Boston.

This enter-at-your-own-risk bar had to close for one hour by law. It closed at sunrise for that hour. Bikers, gamblers, sailors, gay and straight would head outside, watch the sun rise, head back inside and continue. Michael continued by ordering a shot of tequila. The bartender brings something that looks like a shot. "This isn't tequila," Michael mentions.

"Kid, that's a buchi. You either drink that or you ain't getting your shot." He looked Michael in the eye and says, "Because kid, you ain't sleeping here." That was Michael's introduction to Café Cubano.

"What's with the chain-link fence?" Michael asked Jacqueline.

"They like to keep the shrimpers separated from the other patrons."

"Fuck, really?"

Key West was the perfect winter escape. Cape Cod was the perfect summer escape. Michael and his partner Andy had invited some friends to join them for a weekend in Provincetown. They had trailered the catamaran, hoping to get a nice afternoon sail in before Tea Dance. The mast raised, they backed the boat down the launch. The plan was to beach the cat next to the Pied deck and take in some of the show. Michael had seen posters around town and was curious.

Even with the weight of the six passengers, the Nacra sails billowed in a broad reach toward Long Point Light Station. Within sight of the Boatslip sun worshipers, the women became as topless as the men, and grabbed beers from the cooler. Michael was sure they were breaking a few laws, but this was P-town.

Established as a station in 1826, Long Point Light still guides boats, with its green light and foghorn, into Provincetown Harbor from the tip of the peninsula. An early settlement, a military post, saltworks, and an oil factory are all long gone. The only surviving structures out at Long Point are the lighthouse, the oil house, and to the south on a small hill, an old wooden cross.

With a nice beach and a view of the Pilgrim Monument in the distance, the sailors decided to go ashore and eat the sandwiches bought at Far Land Provisions. With the ghost village behind them, the six put down towels and started in on their lunches. Michael loved reading about Provincetown history, so he knew that on this roughly one hundred fifty acres, the Point had been home to thirty-eight fishing families. "Hard to believe there was a post office, a bakery, and a school here in the 1800s. I think I read that there were two hundred adults and sixty children."

"Can't imagine what winters were like. What happened to them?" asked Jill.

"Yeah, it was really hard living out here. Families began to leave mid-1850s. They took their houses with them. Floated them across the harbor."

"That's what those blue plaques are on the houses in town. They're called floaters," added Andy. "Oh shit! We should get going. Might take us a while to get to the Pied, depending on the wind."

Back on the water, they all waved to the passengers on one of the Dolphin vessels as it headed out in search of whales. With the sails in good trim, they were heading toward the rainbow flag dead ahead.

The hulls slid and stopped in the sand. They could hear Carole King's *So Far Away*, accompanied by the flapping of the mainsail as it was quickly lowered. Michael was hoping to hear more from *Tapestry*. Folding chairs had been set up on the dance floor and they grabbed six in the front. Barefoot and dripping salt water on the floor, The Bear gave them a welcoming smile. She hit the triad A major chord and everyone knew they would be singing about feeling like a natural woman soon.

The Bear followed with some Linda Ronstadt that had everyone reliving their own past relationships. Anthony and his boyfriend holding hands, a random kiss, madly in love. The sequence of songs in the set was interpreted as a storyteller. Wondering *When Will I Be Loved* after being mistreated. *It's So Easy* to fall in love by breaking all the rules. I *Don't Know Much* but I'm going to love you for a *Long Long Time*. Finally, after being worked over real good, *Poor Poor Pitiful Me*. Through the power of the contralto to soprano range, she makes the sailors feel they can overcome anything.

Knowing they have to get the boat back to the launch so they could get to dinner, Michael sent a Long Island Iced Tea to his new favorite singer. As the waitress points to Michael, he said "We'll be back tomorrow."

The mainsail is hoisted and hulls floated. They catch a breeze and hear the Mama Cass classic

Make Your Own Kind of Music. They all join in, even if nobody else sings along.

Michael loved the stainless steel panels, the porcelain enamel, glass blocks, terrazzo floors, Formica, and neon sign trim of a classic New England diner. The Blue Diner in the Leather District, Victoria's Diner on Massachusetts Ave, the Rosebud in Davis Square, the Deluxe Diner in Watertown, and Betsy's Diner in Falmouth were some of his favorites, all great places for corned beef hash or macaroni and cheese. But Patrick Belanger's Flash in the Pan on Route 1, north of Boston, prepared duck three ways, the best he had ever tasted. Michael and Andy became regular customers at this counterintuitive concept of a fine dining diner.

They were also regular customers of Susan, a bartender at Fritz, the neighborhood gay bar down the street from their apartment. After a walk to the Esplanade they decided to get a beer and watch the game. Sitting at the bar, "So what do you feel like doing tonight?"

"Wanna go to Flash in the Pan?" Michael asked. "I'm craving some of Patrick's duck."

"Sure, that would be great, it's been a while. We can call him when we get home."

Overhearing while she was pouring, Susan laughed. "I could call him for you. Pat is my husband!"

"You're kidding! We had no idea," Andy said.

"I was just going to call him anyway. What time?"

"How about seven?" Andy got a nod from Michael, as he headed to the bathroom. Taking advantage of Michael's absence, "His thirtieth birthday is coming up. Do you think I could book the Flash for a Sunday surprise party?"

"Of course, hon! Patrick would love that. I'll mention it to him, and you can call him this week to talk about the menu." They quickly changed the subject as Michael returned to his barstool.

Menu set, invitations sent, and secret kept, Michael was expecting a quiet, intimate dinner at his favorite restaurant. Missing the first clue from the parking lot, "Oh wow! The Hat Sisters are here," he said. Andy smiled, seeing the two Seuss-like birthday cake hats through the diner windows.

Everyone yelled "Surprise!" as the Hat Sisters lip sync to Madonna's *B-Day Song*, spanking each other to the beat. Absolutely hysterical. Susan made some classic cocktails, perfectly paired with the hors d'oeuvres on the bar.

Time for Patrick's passion for food and showmanship, the Salade de Isles was plated. From the French Caribbean, on a bed of lettuce were prawns, crab, pineapple, mango, avocado, and grapefruit. The pre-selected entrees of either Patrick's duck, Coq au Vin, or Sole Meuniere was then served. And finally, a chocolate truffle torte with an eau-de-vie de Mirabelle plum after-dinner digestif. And because it was a Sunday night, the birthday party beat moved on to the Metro, where they danced through last call, certainly making Madonna a happy girl.

Michael and Andy had been together for six years. They both remember first hearing about gay men getting sick early in their relationship. They were beginning to lose friends and hearing about acquaintances dying from AIDS, much to the indifference of the Reagan administration. They always participated in the Gay Pride parades in Boston as a celebration of progress and the fight for equality, but the National March on Washington was different. Over three quarters of a million participated in "The Great March". The AIDS Memorial Quilt was displayed for the first time on the National Mall to highlight the scale of the epidemic. Just as the Vietnam Memorial close by, the Quilt entraps the visitor and is emotionally devastating.

Anthony's boyfriend Dan had died and they were looking for his panel. Dan's mom had sewn the memories, and there he was sitting in his lifeguard chair, so handsome and healthy. Growing up on the coast of Maine, JFK's quote "We are tied to the ocean. And when we go back to the sea, whether it is to sail or to watch – we are going back to whence we came," was stitched under the photograph. When Michael saw the picture of the six friends on the catamaran, he joined the collective sobbing and consoling all around him.

The seventh year was one of almost constant bickering and the thought of being single was becoming more and more intriguing. Falling out of love was surprisingly uneventful. Michael's friends seemed more upset about the breakup than he was. For as long as most of them were out, there was always Michael and Andy. Now there was Michael.

While he still enjoyed Provincetown and Key West, his friend Anthony was discovering South Beach. Both had their undergraduate degrees in education, but financial opportunities detoured teaching careers. Both single now, when back in Boston they looked forward to comparing experiences. Over many phone conversations, Anthony would try to convince Michael to join him. "You have to come to South Beach! One night here and you'll never return to Key West."

Anthony decided to move to SoBe, while Michael decided to vacation in Key West again. Staying alone at Simonton Court and heading out to the Copa would be both familiar and unfamiliar at the same time. As he walked down Duval Street toward the club, he could see Jacqueline in the restored theater ticket booth. He quickly glances at the Art of Seduction poster and reaches in to pat her cat. She says "Just one, dear?" looking a bit concerned.

"Just one, for a while," answered with a contented look. She waved him on in, without collecting the cover. He needed to get drunk tonight, so he headed upstairs to see Becky. Tall and strikingly beautiful, she projected a sense of power, strength, and dominance. The balcony was her bar and she knew everyone at her bar. She knew their names and what they drank. However, each drink was a unique libation presented with pride and affection. The tips were very generous.

"Hello Michael, what can I getcha, hon? Crown with a rock?" she asked, making six other concoctions simultaneously.

"Yes, please." She reaches over, kisses him on the cheek, and grabs an old fashioned glass from under the bar. She pours from the distinctive etched glass bottle enough to cover the ice sphere. She adds her signature rainbow gummy worms hanging from a palm tree swizzle stick. He takes a sip and turns to look down at the crowded dance floor. The second Crown had rainbow gummy rings on the swizzle stick. The third had a gummy flip flop pop. A huge Communards fan, when Michael

31

heard *Never Can Say Goodbye*, he was ready to dance.

The Art of Seduction stage performance was a nice change from the usual drag show. Michael was impressed with some of the flamenco steps and one particular dancer. After the show, he went over to chat with Jacqueline and happened to mention it. "That's Diego. He's a sweetheart. When I see you tomorrow night, I want details," she said with a smile and a hug.

Michael wondered how much more Jacqueline knew about him. It didn't take long to find out. Before he knew it, Diego was standing next to him. And before he knew it, they were dancing to the night's last song, Abba's *Lay All Your Love on Me*, disturbingly unprotected. And before he knew it, they were having mimosas at Blue Heaven with the roaming roosters and cats.

They ordered two BLT Bennies with Key West pink shrimp and some of Betty's banana bread. "Have you been to South Beach yet?" Diego asked.

"Not yet. I might visit my friend soon. He just moved there from Boston."

"You will love it. The clubs and music are crazy! I'm thinking we might not be performing here much longer. Miami Beach is so much closer for me and I can be more creative with the acts."

"When were you last in Boston?"

"Not since I started the business here. Maybe I'll come visit you up there in the summer. Escape the heat," he said, but Michael assumed he was just teasing. He thought about the unfamiliar interest in escaping the heat. Escaping the cold was much more desirable.

As an IT consultant, that escape became possible. With some new accounts in South Florida, Michael made plans to stay at Anthony's new apartment. From the airport, traveling the causeway from Downtown to Miami Beach, Michael began to realize he was looking at a place in transition, enchanting and dilapidated, with cruise ships leaving the Port of Miami and homeless sleeping at South Pointe Park. An elderly Jewish population being replaced by a younger gay party crowd.

Michael paid the taxi driver and looked around at the landscaped white and pastel stucco buildings. Dwarf palmettos, pink hibiscus, white flowering marlberry, canna lilies, and tall sabal palms welcomed him to Anthony's courtyard. A neighborhood so vibrant and tropical, very different than the brownstones of the South End of Boston.

The two friends were so happy to see each other, and Anthony couldn't wait to take Michael for a walk to the beach. But first, Anthony needed to take him South Beach shopping. He bought a couple of square cut swim trunks and some sleeveless tees to support a newly opened, gay-owned shop on 13th. On their way to the beach, they stopped to get a shot of wheatgrass juice. Anthony called it a powerful detoxifier and liquid nutrient. Michael had never heard of it but had a feeling he would be drinking it regularly. Damage the body at night, fix it the next day.

Provincetown and Ogunquit had great beaches, but they were nothing like South Beach. House trance from the night before provided the rhythm for volleyball, rollerblading, and exercise stations. As they crossed Ocean Drive into Lummus Park, Michael tried not to act like a northern tourist on vacation, but like a little boy in a candy store, watching his eyes popping out of his head at the sight of the variety of perfectly sculpted bodies, Anthony was amused. When he found his group of friends, they settled on the fine, white sand and began introductions. Anthony and Carlos were about to become Anthony, Carlos, and Michael. "We've heard a lot about you, Michael. It's great finally meeting you. How long are you here for?" Carlos got up, hugged him and stood next to Anthony.

"At least the month, maybe more depending on work," as he looked at the turquoise and peach art deco lifeguard station. "Damn, I've never seen such beautiful turquoise water. It matches the blue on the lifeguard tower."

"Oh my god everyone, did you hear that sexy Boston accent? We love that down here!" Carlos said as he looked over to the others for agreement. "Come on Michael, let's get you into that beautiful turquoise watta." Michael wasn't sure if he liked Carlos, yet.

The water was so warm, and smelled saltier than Cape Cod Bay. As the three of them waded chest deep, it occurred to Michael that this was their way to gossip without the others hearing. "So what are we doing tonight?" Anthony asked Carlos. Michael quickly discovered that not doing anything was not an option in SoBe. And what you did was go out. Every night. And Carlos knew where.

"Public opening at Bobby's Hombre tonight. I've heard Versace will be there. The Del Rubio Triplets are performing. Should be a great introduction to South Beach for Michael," Carlos laughed.

"The Del Rubio Triplets? I saw them on Oprah singing the Stone's *Satisfaction*. Fucking most bizarre thing I've ever seen!" said Michael.

"And don't forget Pee-wee's Playhouse," added Anthony.

"If that's the most bizarre he's ever seen, he needs to get out more," Carlos says to Anthony.

"Oh, we'll take care of that." Anthony splashes Michael and Michael retaliates.

Born on August 23, 1921, the triplets grew up in the Panama Canal Zone. They were popular night club performers in the 1950s, but became campy interpreters of Devo, Rolling Stones, and the Pointer Sisters. So it somehow seemed appropriate to get a gig at the opening of Hombre. In their very short skirts and blond bouffant wigs, the three sixty-somethings came on stage with acoustic guitars and sang *Whip It, Satisfaction,* and *Neutron Dance.* In a preview of what his SoBe experience would be, Michael met Edith, Elena, and Mildred backstage.

The next day, Michael bought a bike and for its maiden trek explored his new neighborhood. In 1962, eight blocks of Lincoln Road were closed to cars, creating a great place to shop, eat, and people watch. An Art of Seduction poster caught his eye in the window of Jeremiah's Gym, and it looked like Diego would be at the Warsaw Ballroom every week. He would have to ask Anthony about Warsaw.

Michael continued to ride around Lincoln Road until he saw Books & Books, and knew he could live here now. He picked up four books set in Florida, Hemmingway's *To Have and Have Not*, Zora Neale Hurston's *Their Eyes Were Watching God*, Russell Banks' *Continental Drift*, and Harry Crews' *Naked in Garden Hills*.

Down Meridian to Flamingo Park, he thought the park might get interesting later. Further down Meridian, all the way to South Pointe Park, he sat at a bench and watched the ships departing from the Miami Cruise Port. Some would turn east, some west. Onto Ocean Drive, he rode to Lummus Park and sat a while on the wall at the Art Deco District Welcome Center. Twilight would be the best time for a daily swim. He was meeting Anthony and Carlos at the News Café for 2-4-1 happy hour. As he joined them, Carlos asked "How was your ride?"

"Great! I love this place. Oh, I saw a Warsaw poster."

"Warsaw tonight," Carlos stated what he thought was the obvious. They ordered a pitcher and Michael realized he would need a nap later. South Beach evenings didn't begin until after eleven, so he had plenty of time. They ordered happy hour appetizers for dinner. As they dug into the chicken nachos and ceviche with chips, Michael spotted Jacqueline.

"There's Jacqueline over there. Do you think that's her boyfriend?" he said quietly.

"Could be. I'm sure it's complicated though," Carlos said. They thought about that a bit.

"I'm going to say hi, be right back." As Michael stood up, Jacqueline spotted him and waved.

"Well hello dear! Nice to finally see you in South Beach," she says and holds up her hand to be kissed. "Michael, this is Xavier."

"Nice to meet you, Xavier. Will you two be at Warsaw tonight?"

"I'll be at the door working, Xavier is a barback there."

"Oh good, so I'll see you both tonight then. Maybe even see Diego, too." Jacqueline winked at him.

Back at the table, Michael poured another beer. "Yeah, that's complicated. Did you know he's a barback at Warsaw?"

"That's where I've seen him," Anthony said. "OK, let's finish up here. I gotta meet a few people."

"I'll ride around a little more and see you back at the apartment. See you tonight, Carlos."

Anthony wasn't home yet, so Michael took a shower. He propped up the pillows and relaxed on his bed. Time to decide which new book to start. He opened Hurston's *Their Eyes Were Watching God*. Captivated by the first sentence, seeing the cruise ships on the horizon in his mind, yet after only a few pages he felt himself nodding off. Maybe it was the bike ride. Anyway, he needed to take a nap if he was going to be out all night.

No need for an alarm clock. The roar of the Harleys heading toward Ocean Drive ripped him from a deep sleep, interrupting a very weird dream with Jacqueline. Saved by the roar, he sat up in bed, thinking about Boston Anthony, the waiter and assistant promoter. Miami Anthony was an event planner, club promoter, and ecstasy dealer. He thought Anthony had changed somehow. Beginning to realize South Beach did that to people, its beauty and warmth lured unsuspecting dreamers seeking respite from the suffocating expectations of their lives. He seemed to be always working to make sure that happened.

On Michael's second night, Anthony and Carlos were determined to lure him into the Warsaw experience. He quickly learned there was a South Beach fashion which differentiated the locals from the tourists. Once the three were ready, they walked toward the beach.

Marcos worked security at Warsaw and had invited them over for drinks and the usual business transaction. His design talent was evident throughout the ocean view condo, which was also his showroom. He had just completed a sculptural wall treatment using steel mesh and was going to try to sell the idea to a client. Michael also got the feeling Anthony was trying to sell the idea of Marcos to Michael. He was always working.

Next on the to-do-list was a Café Cubano and a pastry at the Washington Street ventanita. Carlos ordered at the walk-up window. Words that describe the Cuban-style coffee also describe the people of Miami and their experiences. Passionate. Bold. Intense. Bittersweet. Michael understood why they brought him there, and said "I've had a buchi at Boca Chica, but this was amazing!" Carlos looked at Anthony, impressed, and ready.

The uniqueness of the Warsaw experience began outside the club. Michael had met Jaime at the Hombre opening. He was working the door, with one hand on the red velvet rope hook. In the past, when Michael saw a line to enter a club, he got in line. So when they continued to walk past the line to Jaime's greeting and release of the hook, Michael felt a rare exceptionalism.

Once inside Warsaw, Michael clung to Anthony as they made a beeline to the bar. The DJ had already started spinning and two go-go boys were about to take their places. He looked around, and initially thought the club was typical, almost ordinary. Without asking what Anthony and Carlos wanted from the bar, "You have a specialty shot?" smiling at the bartender. He continued to look around, for Diego.

"I have something you guys will like," he said, putting three shot glasses on the bar. "Goes down nice and smooth." Michael watched as ice was added to a mixing glass, followed by peach schnapps, Crown Royal, triple sec, and sweet and sour mix. Wearing a black tank top, a good shaking brought the exposed bicep to life. An equal pour, he delivers "Three Water Moccasins, no charge, handsome." Anthony smiled at him as they tilted their heads back, opened their mouths, and let the chilled Moccasins fall down the back of their throats, as three ice cold waters were placed on the bar. Anthony had distributed the small zip lock plastic bags at Marcos's apartment. Stealthily unzipping, capturing the yellowish pill and placing it on their tongues, washing the bitterness down with the cold water would soon add to the communal Warsaw euphoria.

Methylenedioxymethylamphetamine, or MDMA helped pay the rent. XTC, or X, or E, also helped loosen inhibitions. The sense of touch is heightened and a close emotional bond with others is experienced. And music sounds better, so Anthony and Carlos wanted to introduce Michael to David Padilla before the X kicked in. "Let's take a walk around," Carlos said.

They backtracked the beeline and stopped at the edge of the dance floor across from the DJ booth. From this perspective, Michael's first impression of typical or ordinary was dissolving. David wanted to send a message out to the floor through Zimbabwean singer Rozalla. *Everybody's Free to Feel Good*. Knowing that we've been hurting, nevertheless, together we'll be just fine. The laser fan drew them in. They had to dance.

Not sure how long they had been dancing, Michael still knew they needed a water break, so he tapped out. Past the stage, they ascended the unsecured VIP metal stairs. They sat on a sofa that Madonna and her entourage probably had recently partied. With the same service, a waiter delivered three Perriers with limes. Up at the same level as the industrial catwalk and dance floor lighting, Michael felt both separated from and encompassed by the Ballroom, missing the communal experience below but noticed that the wall surrounding them looked like something Marcos would have created. Sandwiched on the leather sofa, as the enhanced caresses and deep base surged through his slouched body, he looked at Anthony and said, "Unbelievable." Carlos smiled.

With each descending step, they rejoined The Machine's house. The residents were under this skilled turntablist's control. The three moved to the side of the booth, waiting to interrupt the required concentration, as Michael watched in awe. David, taking advantage of a long instrumental track, came over to say hello. Carlos introduced Michael, and that began the tradition of a wink or a wave or a nod when they saw each other.

The tour almost completed, Michael stood and took it all in. With the dance floor in front of him and the bathroom behind him, this darker space was the opportune cruising spot. Michael loved to cruise, and he was good at it. But tonight he would behave himself. Being on XTC is different than getting drunk. This was a night to discover this place, at this time, together. Experience the ebb and flow through David's music, together. An awareness of the synergy of light and that music, together. And a gradual comedown at sunrise, together. David ends with *I Will Survive*, and the three decide to watch the sun come up over Biscayne Bay on Carlos's balcony. Michael understood now.

Halloween would start mid-afternoon. The temporary dressing room of a long table and mirror was set up in the space outside their bathroom. Cleanly shaven, Carlos arrived barely able to contain his excitement. This was his idea. Michael was a bit apprehensive. Anthony was confident they would impressively pull it off, with some help.

Jacqueline met them at Merle's Closet on Lincoln Road. "OK boys, we don't have much time! Let's find something stunning for each of you," she said, as she professionally searched the racks. A short black sequined number for Michael. Bob Mackie inspired stretch pants and chain link top for Carlos. A Grace Jones one-piece black bra with straps to the leather shorts for Anthony. And of course, the most striking, painful pumps Jacqueline could match with each outfit. Then the hair. A short blond bob for Michael. Long straight black for Carlos. Jacqueline looked at Anthony, "No wig for you. I'll do your hair."

Back at the dressing table, Jacqueline began her instruction. "First, the three of you, go into the bathroom and clean your faces twice, getting into those pores. Then use the toner with a cotton pad." At each station, Jacqueline had arranged the creams, oils, powders, brushes, and lipsticks. Each shiny face had his own assigned seat.

Using the pad of her ring finger, Jacqueline pat a little eye cream and gently massaged it around all six eyes. "Next, boys, take the moisturizer and apply in an upwards and outwards motion. Remember, moisturizing is not an option!" she insisted. "And remember that make-up is a cover-up, and the correct order is important for a flawless wear of your foundation and concealer." Michael had no idea what she was talking about, but wondered if they would be able to successfully conceal their true selves throughout the evening.

The limo was scheduled to pick them up at six o'clock. Jacqueline had a lot more work to do. Primer, foundation, concealer, powder, bronzer then blusher, eyeshadow and eyeliner then mascara, lipstick, and finally penciling the eyebrows. Looking at her watch, "Girls, I think we have time for a drink!"

On Ocean Drive, when the driver opened the limo door, it was the legs that first got noticed. Once in the restaurant, Michael realized he should have rehearsed the legs. Jacqueline leaned over and whispered into his ear, "Michael darling, that's not how a lady sits. Close those knees!"

Then it was off to the Cameo on Washington Ave. The martinis were delicious, stupefying and numbing, except for their feet. Watching the powerful En Vogue drag performance of *Free Your Mind*, Michael had a new-found admiration for moving in stilettos. With pumps in hand, he walked the few blocks home to change into his jeans, wash his face and feet, and went to Warsaw.

Early South Beach mornings were Michael's favorite time of the day. Sometimes it was walking home from after-hours, but mostly it was rollerblading to the beach while Ocean Drive slowly got ready for the day to come. Sanitation workers in the back alleys and power washers on the sidewalks along with modeling shoots and the lone metal detector walking on the sand, all taking advantage of everyone still sleeping.

Michael sat on the Lummus Park wall drinking his coffee, thinking this was going to be an exceptional Saturday night. Anthony and Carlos had been talking about this anniversary party for weeks. Although he knew it probably wasn't true, it seemed that all this early morning activity was preparation for tonight.

He took off his rollerblades and walked toward the edge of the wet sand from the receding tide, where he dropped his backpack and clothes. Some called it sea lice but it was actually the larvae from the thimble jellyfish that caused him to swim naked. Sea bather's eruption is an itchy rash from the larvae when they get trapped inside your bathing suit and begin to sting. Michael would have none of that, plus the warm, salt water felt amazing on his unencumbered body.

Back on his blades, the morning Miami sunshine on his salty, sweaty skin told him it was

45

going to be a hot one. He couldn't wait to get home and take a cool shower, but thought he'd first stop at Playa Café on Washington and get a couple of guava and cream cheese filled pastelitos for breakfast and Cuban sandwiches for lunch.

Anthony was awake, in the shower, and not alone. Michael started the coffee and wondered if this was someone new and if he should have gotten three pastelitos. "Good morning guys, coffee's brewing!" He wanted Anthony to know he was home.

"Thanks, Michael," answered over the running water. "We'll be right out." He wanted Michael to know he had a guest. Michael put out a third coffee cup and cut the pastries, but turned out it wasn't necessary. Anthony's latest conquest was drop-dead gorgeous. "I'm running late for a meeting," Anthony opened the door. "Will you be at Warsaw tonight?"

"I will. Hope to see you there," getting in one last kiss.

Michael knew there was no meeting. "Wow!"

"Yeah, but the caboose seems to be pulling the engine!"

"A lot of that down here." They both laughed and poured some coffee. "The pastelitos are from Playa, and lunch in the fridge."

"Nice. I'll go to the gym and meet you back here for lunch. What you got for plans?"

"Laundry and some reading." Michael still thought it was strange that the washer and dryer were outside in the back alley, and sometimes used by nonresidents. "Definitely a nap this afternoon."

"I'll make some sauce and we can have pasta for dinner tonight. I'll invite Carlos."

Body hair was unacceptable in SoBe. Superfluous fur needed to be waxed, shaved, clipped, tweezed, and trimmed. New England winters allowed for a temporary cessation, but Florida winters kept Michael unnaturally smooth. No one wanted to see back hair on the beach or the dance floor, and certainly no one wanted to stop what they were doing to fish hair from their mouth. "You need to do some manscaping down there," a bedroom guest once observed. The clippers would overheat sometimes, so Michael would start the trimming early today, just in case there was a phase two. He did a zero guard clipping. Not as smooth as shaving, but it was a hell of a lot more comfortable days later. Impatient with the sun's highlighting, he helped it along with a bit of peroxide, showered and then took that nap.

Michael woke to the aroma of Anthony's sauce. The simmering of the garlic, onion, and plum tomatoes was the alarm to get out of bed. In the kitchen, they agreed the only thing better was the smell of freshly brewing Baby's Private Buzz from Key West. Michael read the bag, "The Last Legal High!"

"Carlos is on his way. He's made dessert."

Just as the carafe filled, Anthony buzzed Carlos in. "Damn, it smells good in here!" as his Drakkar Noir was added to the mix. Michael poured the coffees as Carlos took some paper towels to absorb the sweat from his face and torso. "My mom used to say it's like the breath of hell out there."

"What's in the box?" Anthony asked for both of them.

"Flan cake. It's flan, but it's a cake," continuing to wipe the sweat. "Delicious and easy, just like me!"

"Well, we agree about the easiness. We'll let you know about the deliciousness," Anthony said, through the laughing. Michael could tell this was going to be a fun night.

Carlos offered to clean up while Michael and Anthony got ready. Michael had cut the sleeves off a black shirt he bought in Provincetown a few years ago. A pair of button fly 501s and Doc Martins became his club uniform. The sleeveless shirt with some dog tags and a chain belt was the SoBe differentiation from Boston. He took a look at his ass in the mirror and passed inspection.

Back in the living room, Anthony was already counting and distributing the beige pills into the mini zip lock bags. Michael wondered if they would take the Schedule 1 drug in the safety of the apartment or wait until they got to Warsaw. "I wonder what Scott is up to these days?" he asked.

"I know! I remember he used to call this window or his low-calorie martini or Adam," Anthony said. "You would call me when he returned from New York. The first time I used X was his stuff. He would include directions in each packet."

"A psychotherapist, he trained other therapists in the use of MDMA. Depression, substance abuse, relationship problems, premenstrual syndrome, and autism were some of the disorders Adam therapy treated. And then Studio 54 and Paradise Garage discovered it."

"And here we are, about to have the time of our lives. Thanks, Scott!" Carlos said. "Let's get going. I want to stop for a cafecito." Down the stairs and into the courtyard, they were hit by that breath of hell Carlos told them about.

The line went further down Española Way than Michael had ever seen, so he felt extra exceptional when they walked past it to Jaime as he raised the red velvet rope. But no one got past Jacqueline. "Hello Michael," she winked at him and collected the ten dollar cover. Michael reached in, kissed Jacqueline on her hand, and patted the cat.

They worked their way to their corner of the bar and looked around the club in awe of the new industrial interior. Anthony looked around one more time and put that all-too-familiar bitter tasting pill in Michael's mouth. David was soon to take control, as the volume of the deep tribal base suddenly intensified.

Carlos looked surprised when Diego joined them and gave Michael a hug and kiss. "They have a history," Anthony informed Carlos. "They met in Key West. Jacqueline introduced them." Carlos didn't need the details.

Diego looked into Michael's eyes. "I see you'll be having a fun night," as he noticed how Michael's pupils had taken over the diameter of the hazel. "Glad the penis hasn't collapsed," he said with a concerned look, then a smile. "See you later I hope. Back to work." Michael thought about how he really liked Diego, but knew Diego only liked Diego.

The waves of sweat and a warm rush merged with the visuals of drag queens and go-go boys, laser light-fans, surreal sideshow performances, freakish, dreamlike. As Anthony washed down pill number two, Michael felt a chill and needed to stay close to his friend. "It's OK if you want to hold me," he hears Anthony say. Alone together, a fantasia with hundreds of others, all doing exactly what they want to be doing, more than anything else in the world.

"This feels amazing," Michael said. "This place," pausing, in a state of altered consciousness, complete euphoria, "with you." Carlos joined them as the music surged through the hundreds with that tribal rhythm, warmth and intimacy.

"We need to dance." Anthony leads his two friends to join David's unbounded trance, until the E7 arpeggio chord is rolled up the piano and back down again.

The Bear is illuminated in a flood of white light. The Anniversary Party is almost over. In that powerful, clean voice Michael remembers from Provincetown, she sings Gloria Gaynor's *I Will Survive*. A much needed message of personal strength and defiance, from which fear turns into a resolution of survival, and love.

The house lights come on to a round of applause, followed by security forcefully suggesting that everyone finish their drinks and head toward the door. But everyone isn't done. After-hours begins now. The crowd hangs outside while old and new friends decide how they will spend the early morning. "Up for the Deuce?" Anthony asked, as they head to 14th Street.

ANTHONY

Anthony hated the smell of dead fish, but he loved the smell of garlic. His grandfather, father and brothers smelled of dead fish and his grandmother, mother and sisters smelled of garlic. His family's fishing boats and trawlers work out of the Custom House Wharf. His family's home is in Portland's India Street neighborhood, or Little Italy. *La famiglia e per sempre.*

During many teenage summers, Anthony would be sternman on his brother's lobster boat. By sunrise, with his older brother at the helm, they would be out locating their buoys in Jeffreys Bank. Eight plastic-coated metal traps along a stringer were attached to each buoy. Anthony would prep the bait until they reached one. He would quickly grab the line with a hook and feed it through the winch. A hydraulic hauler would then drag each trap out of the water, and they would sift through the catch, looking for keepers. When all eight traps are pulled, he lowers the line into the water and the newly baited traps on the stern fly off one by one, to be pulled again the next day. And the next day, and the next day, and the next day.

The hell with family, Anthony knew this was not the life he wanted. He graduated from the University of Maine with a degree in Elementary Education. Not sure when and where he wanted to teach, so that summer he got a job as a waiter and hung around with friends at Crescent Beach, many from Cape Elizabeth. The mile-long sandy beach is part of a state park with sand dunes, picnic area with a snack bar, restrooms and cold water showers, and lifeguards.

Anthony wasn't out to most of these friends yet, except for Tara. Best friends since elementary school, they had no secrets, and they trusted each other with those secrets. "You seem very distracted today," she said, applying some sunscreen on his back.

"What's his story?" looking over to the lifeguard chair.

"He just graduated from Orono, too. I'm surprised you don't know him," she said. "His name is Dan and he has a girlfriend."

"How do you always know this stuff?"

"How do you not?" she laughed. "Let's take a walk and invite him to the Pirate Party." The crescent shaped beach is an easy one to work, and is popular with families because of its gentle surf. No one was in the ice cold water, so they approached the chair. "Hi there! I'm Tara, and this is my friend Anthony." He hopped down to shake their hands.

"Nice meeting you," he said smiling. The white zinc oxide on his nose matched his perfect white teeth. "You went to Orono, right?"

"Yeah, I just graduated," Anthony said.

"Me too. I thought you looked familiar. Were you a member of Alpha Sigma Phi?"

"Yeah, I was an officer, bad memories." Anthony didn't like talking about it. "I loved Greek life, but the long-established frats have a history of homophobic reprisals." Tara looked at him and shook her head. "Anyway, have you heard about the Pirate Party?"

Looking out at the offshore island, "It's out on Richmond. You should join us," Tara said.

"I'd love to. Can I bring a couple of friends?"

"Of course, just make sure they have a costume and like to drink! We'll go from here to the dock, starting at 10ish," Anthony said. "We should let you get back to work."

"No problem. Come hang anytime," again with that smile.

Walking back, Tara said "Maybe he doesn't have a girlfriend."

"Not any more he doesn't!"

Dan would drive almost two hours to Boston when he needed to get away. After getting a room at the Chandler Inn, he would have a beer downstairs at Fritz. He always felt welcome at the small, gay, neighborhood sports bar, perhaps because they thought he would be a great addition to their softball team. "What can I get ya, hon?"

"Sam Adams please." His choice in Boston, they didn't have it in Portland.

"So how's Portland treating you these days?" Susan asked, pouring the dry hopped lager.

"Not too bad, pretty progressive but it can be such a small town."

"Yeah, sucks everyone knowing your business."

"Yup, I can come down here, go crazy, and no one will ever know."

"That the plan for tonight?"

"Heading to the 12. Might grab last call here. Will you still be on?"

"I'll be here."

"Great. We'll do some B-52s to end the night!" Susan builds this impressive classic creamy, layered shooter, armed with Kahlua, Baileys and Grand Marnier that Dan loved. The separation had something to do with the relative densities of the liqueurs.

Rather than take a taxi, Dan decided to walk down Tremont Street to Mass Ave to 1270 Boylston Street. Passing the South End brownstones, Symphony Hall, and Olmsted's Back Bay Fens with the oldest remaining war-time Victory Gardens, he thought someday he would live here. Hungry, he walked up the three flights of stairs to the roof deck, lit by the lights from Fenway Park. He had to have the sausage, peppers and onion sandwich, perfect with another beer.

He grabbed a table and took the first bite. Damn, that's good, he thought. The deck didn't have many tables and chairs, so two guys came over and one asked "Mind if we join you?"

"Of course not!" Dan was surprised at the friendliness. This was more like Portland than Boston.

"My name is Michael, and this is Andy."

"Hi, I'm Dan," he reached out to shake their hands. "Do you guys live in Boston?"

"Yeah, we live in the South End, on Tremont Street. You?

"Portland, but I hope someday to move here. I probably walked by your place from Fritz. I love the South End."

When they finished eating, they went downstairs to the second floor to dance until last call. At the end of the night, people liked to hang outside a while. "You two should come up to Portland next weekend for the Pirate Party," Dan said. "I think I have something you can wear from past years."

"Sure, that sounds like lots of fun!" Michael said. They exchanged phone numbers and walked toward Mass Ave.

"I feel like being bad, guys. Think I'll go in and see what I can find," Dan said, heading into the Fens Victory Gardens.

"OK Dan, we'll see you next weekend. And you be safe." And off he went, disappearing into the tall reeds.

Everyone was looking forward to the annual Pirate Party on Richmond Island, with decorated raft races, swashbuckler costumes, volleyball, a clambake, fire pit, and lots of drinking. The launch tender from the Portland Yacht Club will transport everyone to the island and once everyone and everything is on Richmond, the island caretaker will greet them and go over the rules and regulations.

The island maintains a "pack it in/pack it out" policy which means all trash, garbage and waste, including human waste, must be removed. "Get your WAG Bags here!" Tara announced, as each pirate lands onshore. The Waste Alleviation and Gelling Bag kit contains an outer zip-close disposal bag, a waste collection bag with treatment powder, toilet paper and a hand sanitizer towelette.

Anthony saw Dan with a couple of friends. They looked a bit baffled by the Wag Bags, so he heads over to help, but he actually really wanted to hang with Dan. "You guys look confused!" he said.

"So what do we do when we have used them?" Dan asked.

"Just toss it in the box labeled 'Out' over there."

They nodded. "This is Michael and Andy, the friends I told you about from Boston."

"Hey guys, nice to meet you. You want to help with the clambake?"

"Sure, just tell us what to do," Andy said. This was their first beach clambake.

"Great. Grab a shovel, a bucket and a beer."

Anthony first needed to decide where the high tide shore line would be and they started to dig down three feet. Then they went on a quest for rounded stones, driftwood and seaweed, and lined the bottom of the pit with the stones and seaweed and placed a metal grill on top. They brought some wooden grilling planks and used them and the driftwood to get a good fire going, and added more stones, letting the fire burn for a few hours, adding more wood when needed.

Anthony and Dan decided to take a walk exploring the island, leaving Michael and Andy to keep watch of the pit fire. Tara was playing volleyball, but saw the two of them disappear down the perimeter path, and smiled. "I hope we see the island's sheep herd," Anthony said.

"I look out at this island every day and this is the first time I've been here. I know it's owned by the Sprague Corporation, along with Crescent Beach State Park. The family is highly respected for being good stewards of this beautiful place." And Dan added, "Plus, their name is on my paycheck!"

The island's ecosystems support a variety of wildlife. Deer, horned owls, blue herons, brown hawks, piping plovers and swans might be seen while walking from beach to beach. During their walk, Anthony and Dan talked about family, travel, music, politics, movies, friends, pets, workout routines, school, clothes and food. From beach to beach they discovered their common deep connection to the Maine coast and possibly each other. Without a doubt, it was a transformative two miles.

Rejoining the increasingly drunken pirates, the pit was glowing with heat. They added one more layer of wet, sizzling seaweed and it was time for the food. Potatoes, corn, onions, carrots, linguica sausages, clams, mussels, and the lobsters are layered with more seaweed. The four guys cover the pit with a canvas, soaked with seawater, and anchor it down with rocks so the steam doesn't escape. Everyone will have to wait at least two or three more hours.

This was a great time for the raft races! Single and team pirates had been taping, hammering, sawing, tying, painting and inflating for about an hour. It was beginning to look like a Jimmy Buffett pre-concert parking lot. There were no rules other than the damn things needed to float with at least one person on board. Hopefully, some would even cross over the finish line.

They pulled the canvas off the pit. The lobsters were that done-red. The quahog shells were open. There was a sweet corn and onion smell in the air. The potatoes and sausages perfectly cooked, with lots of melted butter and ice cold beer. It didn't suck being a pirate.

Anthony and Dan found a great apartment in Portland's East End, in the Munjoy Hill neighborhood. Near the Eastern Prom, with a view of Casco Bay, they would often bike ride or run to the historic promenade. The 1.5-mile park was designed by the Olmsted Brothers, the sons of Frederick Law, and has baseball fields, basketball and tennis courts. Sometimes they would go for a quick swim at the East End Beach.

The cold water could be rejuvenating, but often it was just painful. Relieved to be soaking up the warming rays of the sun, they talked about their upcoming Provincetown trip. "Michael said he is bringing the catamaran," Anthony sounded concerned. "Have you ever been on one of those?"

"Yeah, a friend from Scarborough has a Hobie Cat. It can get pretty intense out on the butt-bucket harnesses."

"Once in a while I see a cat flying by when I'm at Ogunquit Beach. Seems kinda scary to me!" Anthony said, not sure he wanted that experience.

"Well, no worries, there's always Herring Cove Beach and the Boatslip," Dan said.

But he did worry. Everyone worried these days. Worried that their pasts would catch up with them. Worried that a cold was more, that a lump would grow, that a lesion would multiply. Worried that friends would disappear, that family would disown. But mostly he worried about Dan.

The sight of the Truro Flower Cottages was worth the tedious, four-hour drive. Built in 1931, each of the twenty-two identical, beachfront, 420-square-foot cottages is named after a flower. Leaving Route 6, with the rolling sand dunes behind them and the Pilgrim Monument in the distance on Route 6A, Provincetown was minutes away.

It was already time for Tea. Anthony and Dan, Michael and Andy, and Andy's cousin Jill and her girlfriend would join the hundreds and hundreds of sunbaked, freshly showered carousers at the Boatslip Beach Club. The six walked down the slight slope from Commercial Street, through the leather privacy curtains to pay the cover, past the heated pool and dance floor, and onto P-town's largest waterfront deck, where they were quickly served cocktails by one of the waiters in white short shorts.

"We'll be sailing out there tomorrow," Michael said, looking out at Provincetown Harbor. "That's Long Point and Cape Cod Bay on the other side."

"As long as it's not too windy!" Anthony said. Michael was hoping for at least 10-15 knots so the six of them could experience a fun, upright experience. Any more than that could be trouble.

Looking back, Long Island Iced Teas could be trouble, too. When they heard Neil Tennant's voice looking back at everything fun, it was time to dance. The six Catholics joined the rest of the sinners on the dance floor, with the Pet Shop Boys reminding everyone that everything they've ever done, *It's a Sin*. And Anthony didn't care because you have to live your life. All the arms were up in the air for Ultra Nate's *Free*. Just as Tea reaches its peak and the crowd is pulled in, the celebratory chorus is over. The crowd is then pushed out onto Commercial Street.

The vodka, gin, rum, tequila and Triple Sec encouraged the *Off to See the Wizard* skipping down Commercial into the Pied Piper. The wizardry of DJ Maryalice's disco house and Top 40 dance music seamlessly continued the party. Anthony knew they were too drunk to go out to a restaurant, so they decided to stop dancing and grab a burger out on the Pied deck. The waterfront grill provided a much needed interlude so they could continue the frivolity without heading back to their rooms and passing out.

"So where to next?" Michael asked.

"I think we will close the Pied and then meet you boys at Spiritus for a slice," Jill said.

"Let's go to the A-House," Anthony suggested. The others nodded.

"See you at Spiritus with the hordes!" Andy said to Jill, always looking out for his cousin. "We'll meet you out front here."

With the third cover of the day paid, they entered the packed, historic building. Built in 1798 by Daniel Pease, it was operated as a tavern until his death of cholera in 1834. Eugene O'Neil and Tennessee Williams hung out at the Atlantic House in the 1920s. Nina Simone, Eartha Kitt, Ella Fitzgerald, and Billie Holiday sang in the cabaret when Reggie Cabral bought and managed the A-House starting in 1950, and made the discretely gay bar the most popular and only year-round dance club in Provincetown. And they danced until last call.

The Pied Piper, Crown and Anchor, Gifford House, Boatslip, and A-House all empty out onto Commercial Street toward Spiritus Pizza. The late night hangout is open until 2 a.m., an hour after the bars close. Slinging the perfect slice since 1971, it has become the traditional end-of-the-night gathering spot. Perfectly synchronized, Jill and Pat met their four sweaty, drunk and hungry friends under the Pied sign. "We'll go get in line. How many slices?" Anthony asked, and counted eight.

"This might take a while!" Commercial Street was sidewalk to sidewalk people for two blocks. Anthony and Dan returned eventually with two slices in each hand. "Fuck that was crazy, but worth it!" Anthony said, distributing the still-hot pizza. And they people-watched until the last bites.

The mid-morning aroma of brewing coffee waft through the house, slowly waking the hungover guests. Not feeling all that great on land, Anthony wondered how he would feel later on water, even without the hangover. Michael was trying to get everyone moving and bacon was a foolproof motivator. Add to that some scrambled eggs and lemon custard pastries from the Portuguese Bakery and everyone finally seemed ready for a day sail. "We'll go get the boat rigged," Michael said. "Why don't you stop at Far Land Provisions on the way to the launch and grab some beer and sandwiches."

Launching from the beach with the sheets out, they all followed Michael's instructions. Pushing the boat out into the water until knee deep, "OK everyone, jump aboard!" And immediately at a close reach, the wind was hitting the boat between the bows and the beam and they were flying across Provincetown Harbor toward Long Point. A few tacks and they were on the Bay side, with the lighthouse guiding them ashore. "One of the joys of sailing a Nacra is the ability to land the boat on the beach," Michael said, as the hulls slid onto the sand.

65

They put down towels and Anthony opened the cooler. The Far Land sandwiches are named after favorite P-town locations. "We got two Race Points, two Long Points, and two Herring Coves," Anthony announced. The roast beef, Swiss and horseradish sauce went to Michael and Andy. The smoked turkey, cheddar and horseradish sauce went to Jill and Pat. The roast beef, garlic herb spread and roasted red pepper went to Anthony and Dan.

They talked about the fishing families that lived out on the Point in the 1800s until it became too difficult to make a living and floated their houses across the harbor. They watched a 60-foot steel-hulled scalloper and groundfish trawler returning to MacMillan Wharf, and Anthony thought about his family, and how difficult it was for them to make a living.

As one of the Dolphin vessels passed them heading out in search of whales, they decided it was time to head in toward the rainbow flag at the Pied. The hulls slid and stopped on the sand, this time with the Pied deck to their left and Carole King's *So Far Away* enticing them up the stairs and into the back entrance. And there she was, The Bear. Her voice, like her presence, was big and beautiful. Singing one of the best ballads ever written, she filled the room. They sat feet away, connected, yet she seemed so far away, disconnected. And then Aretha took over, and damn wasn't there someone that made The Bear feel like a natural woman again!

Anthony called Michael and Andy. "I think you should get here as soon as you can," his voice cracked. "He is very sick and the doctors don't think he will last the week." They quickly packed and drove to Portland.

A few weeks earlier, Dan had a dry cough and difficulty breathing after his morning swims. After a sleepless night with chills, Anthony brought him to their neighborhood clinic. Later that day, he was admitted to Maine Medical Center, where he was diagnosed with pneumocystis pneumonia. The ICU staff were puzzled at how quickly PCP stole his youthful vitality as his condition went from fair to serious to critical in a matter of days.

Dan's mom knew it would be important for him to see his friends, and as the HIV epidemic grew, the Medical Center's ICU humane policy allowed for that. Anthony and she met Michael and Andy in the family lounge. "Hello boys, thanks for coming," hugging them. "I've heard so much about you from Dan." Anthony hugged next, trying unsuccessfully to keep that pent-up sorrow and anger from coming to the emotional surface. Michael held his friend tight until the spasms subsided. There was never a shortage of tissues in the family lounge, so

Michael pulled a few for Anthony, which brought a smile.

"I'll bring you guys in to see Dan one at a time," Anthony said. "Don't be alarmed at all the machines and tubes and beeping. And he's lost a lot of weight, so he looks gaunt. But this is a good day, so I'll be able to take off the oxygen mask so he can talk." The automatic doors buzzed open, Anthony and Michael went in, while Andy stayed with Dan's mom. Anthony introduced Michael to the nurses as they approached his bed. He gently placed his hand on Dan's arm and he opened his eyes at the touch. The sight of Michael and Anthony calmed the initial panic shown through his masked eyes, struggling to breath. "Let me take this off for a few minutes, OK?" Dan nodded.

"It's good to see you Michael," Dan said, coughing. "How's Andy?"

"He's entertaining your mom."

"Oh, I'm sure that's an interesting conversation!" He tried to laugh, but just coughed more, which brought in one of the nurses.

"Here Dan, you need to keep this on," she said, returning the mask to his face. When the nurse left the room Anthony took the mast off again. The mechanical ventilation would continue to be noninvasive per Dan's wishes, even though his blood oxygen saturation was low and his shortness of breath was severe. He was done fighting and just wanted to go home to Munjoy Hill and look out onto Casco Bay.

A few days later, he got his wish. Dan's family and friends gathered at Munjoy Hill and released his ashes over the Bay. Anthony read from JKF's speech given in Newport, the night before the 1962 America's Cup. "All of us have in our veins the exact same percentage of salt in our blood that exists in the ocean, and, therefore, we have salt in our blood, in our sweat, in our tears. We are tied to the ocean. And when we go back to the sea -- whether it is to sail or to watch it -- we are going back from whence we came." Later that night Dan's mom started to create his quilt panel, with the JFK quote hand-embroidered, the letters stitched into the salty teared fabric.

Anthony wrote a letter to the NAMES Project about Dan and their relationship for the Foundation's archives. He wrote about their first walk together on Richmond Island, his love and dedication to family and friends, and the lives he saved as a lifeguard.

Anthony and Dan had talked so much about moving to Boston, that the pull of its opportunities became fulfilled through a push from Dan's spirit. These were not teaching opportunities, but social and service opportunities that Portland couldn't offer. The South End would offer an escape from the memories. A transition of new experiences was the slap in the face that he needed, and Michael would be a few blocks away, just in case.

Anthony found a third floor apartment on Union Park. The bow-front row houses built of red brick with painted sandstone trim were in one of three squares designed and built in the 1850s. His living room overlooked the two matching cast iron, lotus flower pattern fountains in the center of the park with a row of elm trees on each side. The natural noises of gently splashing water and of birds chirping masked the city sounds on either end of the park.

Ready early for his first day at the restaurant, Anthony sat on his stoop in his black dress pants, white shirt, black tie, and shined shoes. Taking in the senses of his new city, he thought about the history of this place. New York City and Boston stoops were built to raise the parlor floor above the horse manure. When the rains came, a stream of the smelly manure seeped into the basements. Beneath the main stair also happened to be the second entrance for servants and delivery people, away from the wealthy homeowner.

Anthony sat on his stoop thinking about this neighborhood in transition. Gone were the servants, but with the sound of sawing and hammering throughout the South End, the restorations made the contrast between the haves and the have-nots strikingly apparent. So when he stood up and walked down the stairs, he turned left toward Tremont Street and not right toward Washington.

Charles Street was one of his favorite streets in Boston, and now Anthony worked there. Walking from the Public Gardens into the Common, onto Beacon Hill's brownstone-lined Charles Street, he thought the commute to work could not be better. In one of those 1840s restored brownstones was The Hungry I. Tucked just below street level, passersby know this is a special destination. Each of the three small dining rooms, with exposed brick walls illuminated by a fireplace and the glow of candles on every table, is warm and intimate. Upholstered banquettes with embroidered throw pillows help create the cozy atmosphere. Anthony's welcoming personality would add to the charm of this traditional French bistro.

Before opening each night, details in the preparation of some dishes and wine pairings were discussed at the staff meeting with sous-chef Talie. A tasting of specials and changes to the menu provided rehearsal needed for the staff to help in patron decisions, with the goal of diner bliss. Anthony knew the menu and was beginning to know the regulars.

Richard and Stephan always reserved a table by the fireplace. A gay couple from a different time, impeccably dressed and groomed, both were much younger looking than their years together. They valued life's experiences and beauty, evident in Anthony's generous gratuities. Greeting with that dimpled smile, and knowing what the answer would be, "Good evening, gentlemen. Wonderful to see you. Two Sazeracs?"

"Good evening, Anthony. Yes, please," Richard answered.

"I'll be right back with your drinks. I'll tell you about our specials when I return." Anthony placed three Old-Fashioned glasses on the bar. In one of the glasses he muddled a sugar cube with a few drops of water. Added several small ice cubes and some 18 year-old Sazerac rye whiskey. Into both of the other chilled glasses he rolled around a few drops of Nouvelle-Orleans absinthe. Stirred well, he strained into the glass and repeated the muddling, pouring, stirring and straining. Finally, garnished with twists of lemon, delivered to the table.

Anthony would routinely inform them of the specials, but these two were absolute creatures of habit. Richard would choose the lobster bisque fra diavolo followed by the tournedos of beef. Stephan would have the warm quail salade with the carnard l'orange. The entrees were always accompanied with a bottle of reliable spicy Syrah from the Rhone Valley. They would split the opera torte for dessert.

On slow nights, the staff could engage in some fascinating shared conversation with their favorite patrons. Anthony loved learning about Richard and Stephan through their stories. Often comical, sometimes frightening, they kept a low profile as a couple for many decades, just as the gay bars did with their unmarked doors and blackened windows. "Dear, do you remember that night the police raided Napoleon's?" asked Richard.

"Which one?" Stephan looked at Anthony. "I remember a few."

"The night we went out with your sister and her girlfriend."

"Oh yes! They talked about that for years."

The Napoleon Club in Bay Village opened as a speakeasy in 1929 and later operated as an upscale private club with a sizeable gay clientele. Through the 1940s, the club required jacket and tie. In 1952, under new ownership, Napoleon's officially became a gay bar and eventually a piano bar. "We knew there was always a chance of a police raid," Richard began the story. "Sometimes they would just write up the Club for having 'girlie-boys' in there. But sometimes, for whatever reasons, the raids demanded identification and often arrests. So, luckily, this one night we went out with another couple of the opposite sex."

"Gay bars in those days had a system that would warn everyone that a vice raid was about to happen," Stephan said.

"So when we saw the red flashing light we quickly changed dancing partners. I started dancing with Stephan's sister."

"And I started dancing with her girlfriend. I don't even remember what her name was, but I remember the song was Doris Day's *Secret Love*. They saw that Anthony looked puzzled, so they started to sing about their secret love, not secret anymore. So it was no surprise that in one of the most romantic restaurants in all of Boston, others joined in, "shouting from the highest hills" proclaiming their love.

"So what happened next?" Anthony asked.

"Well, the police seemed intent on arresting everyone, and they did, except for us. They thought we were straight!" Richard cut his laughter short. "The next day the Boston Post published the names and occupations of all those arrested... teacher, accountant, doctor, priest, cook, actor, insurance agent, plumber, mechanic, postal worker, waiter, office manager, realtor, bus driver, scientist, photographer, florist, forklift driver, hairdresser, fire fighter, bartender, professor, our neighbors, our friends," he paused. The room went from singing to ruminating. "Some lost their jobs. Families were destroyed."

"And all because some asshole at city hall or police headquarters didn't get paid that week," Stephan added in disgust.

"It's hard to imagine how awful those days were, and yet you guys persisted and fought for us. I love hearing your stories," Anthony smiled.

"Why don't you come over to our place for dinner some night? We have some great photographs of those days," Richard said. "And Stephan makes a great shrimp scampi!"

"I would love to! That sounds wonderful," Anthony said.

"You tell us what night is good for you. We are on Louisburg Square."

"I have Sunday night off."

"Sunday night it is then. Oh, and bring a friend. Here is our address and phone number."

"I'll bring some opera torte for dessert."

"Louisburg Square! Have you seen those townhouses? Of course I want to go to dinner at their place," Michael said. "And Sunday night, we can go out to Metro after. I'm sure they go to bed early," smiling.

"I doubt that. Wait until you meet these guys. They'll probably want to go out to Metro, too."

The Public Garden was alive with new spring plantings and the opening of the swan boats on the lagoon. They continued their walk down Charles Street and took a right onto Mt Vernon Street. Down two blocks on the left, they arrived at one of the most prestigious neighborhoods in the country. The Square itself is an oval park surrounded by an iron fence. The Greek Revival townhouses on Louisburg Square are a vestige of the bygone upper class of Beacon Hill. There had been some talk among the staff about just how wealthy Richard and Stephan are, but when Anthony and Michael arrived at their home, they were astounded.

While the doorbell chimed, Richard greeted them, "Welcome to our home, gentlemen. Please come in." That sense of historic elegance followed them from the iron fence surrounding the oval park into the foyer. "Stephan is preparing dinner. I'm sure you can smell the garlic!"

"Reminds me of home," Anthony said, smiling.

Richard had certainly given their guests a heads-up. As they entered the kitchen, the freshly chopped pungent garlic aroma accompanied the greeting from Stephan, followed by Michael's introduction.

"Nice meeting you, Michael. Cocktail time! Do you like rye?" Richard asked.

"Well, we like Crown Royal," Michael answered and wondered.

"We will make Sazeracs for you for a change."

"That sounds wonderful," Anthony looked at Michael. "Wait until you try this."

"Proceed with caution though," Stephan warned, reminded of a few times they overindulged. They sat overlooking the garden as Richard served the cocktails. "I've always found it coincidental that the Sazerac Coffee House created this drink mid-19th century at around the same time this house was built. Both have been in my family for generations."

"We can relax here a while. Before dinner we'll give you a tour and we thought after dinner we could sit up on the deck," Richard said, placing a cheese tray on the table.

That sense of historic elegance continued throughout the five bedrooms, six full baths, and two half baths. The exquisite detail of the grand paneled library and parlor were of a place and time Anthony and Michael were unfamiliar. They settled in the dining room, of which the cathedral ceiling was jaw-dropping. The unfamiliarity continued with the formal place settings. Anthony counted five forks, four knives, three spoons, and five glasses!

"We haven't used the formal stuff in a long time," Richard said, looking at the puzzled look on Michael's face. "It's simple. Starting with the knife, fork, or spoon that is farthest from your plate, work your way in, using one utensil for each course. The salad fork is on your outermost left, followed by your dinner fork. Your soup spoon is on your outermost right, followed by your beverage spoon, salad knife, and dinner knife."

"Right in front of you is the water goblet, then Champagne flute, red wine glass, white wine glass, and finally the sherry glass," Stephan said. "We should be a bit tipsy by then!"

So they worked their way in over the course of the evening starting with a focaccia al rosmarino and heirloom tomato salad. The broth of the spicy Thai tom yum soup was made from the shrimp shells. The main, shrimp scampi, saffron rice, and asparagus, was deliziosissima! The opera torte with its layered coffee buttercream, chocolate ganache, and Viennois cake along with a cup of smooth lemon-kissed espresso finished the meal.

Napkins back on the table, "Shall we go up to the roof deck?" Richard asked. They ascend to the sixth floor study wet bar for a bottle of Pedro Ximenez sherry, probably the sweetest wine in the world from its raisining in the sun. Carefully carrying the bottle and glasses, they climbed the spiral staircase out onto the deck, where the jaw-dropping recurred. The two-tiered roof deck's views of the Charles River and Boston were dramatic. So weren't Richard and Stephan's stories, which Anthony loved. "Did I ever tell you about the time we partied with Judy Garland?" Richard asked, as they settled into the yellow cushioned lounge chairs.

"No you haven't!" Anthony looked at Michael, then back at Richard waiting for the show to begin. "I'm not surprised though."

"Well," looking disappointed, "we were never at Napoleon's when Liberace played, but after seeing her perform at the Back Bay Theater in May of '68, we decided to head on over for a drink, or two," he smiled. "Judy decided to head on over for more than two."

"Those were crazy years. That poor girl was dead one year after we met her," Stephan shook his head. "But she sure did love us gays, and we loved her."

"She had earlier performed a two-hour concert, but seemed drawn to the piano bar at Napoleon's, as was her last-to-be husband. I'll never forget her singing *For Once in My Life* and *I Can't Give You Anything But Love*. And she paid for all our drinks that night!" Richard remembered, sort of. "Everyone at the piano drank, sang, drank, laughed, drank, and cried along with her. Of course we all wanted to hear about the munchkins, and she didn't disappoint. 'Those little drunk bastards couldn't keep their hands off me!' she slurred, and we laughed so hard we cried."

"That fucking studio pumped her with uppers during the day and downers at night. She was only sixteen," Stephan took a sip of the sweet sherry.

"To Judy, somewhere over the rainbow!" Anthony held up his glass, and the others clinked, echoing the incantation, "To Judy!"

They looked out onto the city skyline and knew they needed to dance. "Sunday night boys!" Stephan tipped his head back, finished the last of the Ximenez. Assuming it was what Anthony and Michael planned, he had called Patrick at the Metro and reserved a VIP booth. "Anthony, I know you're interested in event promotion. I'll introduce you to Patrick tonight. The 'King of Clubs' might have something for you." Stephan quickly spiraled down and spiraled back up. "I got something for us!" The glass vial with a golden spoon attached was passed around a few times, saving some for later.

The taxi stopped at 15 Lansdowne and that night was the end of waiting in club lines for Anthony and his friends. The house base volume kicked them in their chests as they slowly made their way toward the reserved booth. "Good evening, Neil."

"Good evening, Richard, Stephan. How is everyone tonight?" It was Neil's responsibility that the Metro VIPs would want for nothing. He attentively stood at his post wanting, needing, waiting for them to justify his existence.

"We are wonderful, thanks. "This is Anthony and Michael." Introductions done, drink orders done, another pass of the vial done. When Neil returned with the drinks, Michael watched, knowing that Anthony certainly would want for nothing later tonight. Until then, they would dance, wired to Anthony Somerville's *Why*, fighting for their love.

Patrick always checked in on his VIPs. He had to. But with Richard and Stephan he wanted to. They were more entertainment than anything else happening at Metro, more than the go-go boys and girls, the drag queens, the DJs, the singers, and the bands. Boston was becoming home to Patrick, and they knew Boston and its club scene. He respected their experience and trusted their advice. "So Patrick, you still looking for an assistant?" Stephan asked.

"I am, yes. Why you know someone?"

"Well, we think Anthony here would be a perfect promoter for the club," Richard said, confidently.

Looking at Anthony, "Well, you couldn't get a better recommendation. Here's my card. Call my office and arrange a time to come in and we'll talk," Patrick said, distracted. "I have to get backstage. You all enjoy yourselves." And he disappeared into the crowd.

Anthony held a dream in his hand. He reached over and kissed Richard, then Stephan. "Thank you so much guys!"

"You're welcome, Anthony. Just don't fuck it up!" Richard warned. Michael smiled, knowing exactly what he meant.

Hired by the "King of Clubs", Anthony knew he had a lot to learn. Ultimately, his aim as an assistant promoter was to help draw a big crowd for Sunday nights, create a safe and enjoyable atmosphere, attract a loyal following, and to make money for the club. His job description included coordinating and setting up special events, writing, designing, and distributing brochures and posters for those events, and maintaining an event calendar.

Patrick would be demanding reliability, trustworthiness, and a range of skills, including knowledge of popular music and gay culture, good interpersonal skills to manage a network of contacts, and self-discipline. And he remembered Richard's warning, "Just don't fuck it up!"

Anthony was hearing about a dance troupe from Miami and saw an ad in Bay Windows for Tunnel on Twelfth Ave in Chelsea featuring The Art of Seduction. He called Michael. "Got any plans Saturday night?"

"Not yet, why, what you have in mind?"

"We're going to the Tunnel!" Anthony told him. "I'll reserve a room at Chelsea Pines Inn, and don't worry about money, it's a business trip."

"Holy shit!"

"I know, I love my job."

After the four hour drive, Anthony and Michael settled into the Donna Reed room. Each of the twenty-four rooms at the Chelsea Pines is dedicated to a different movie star. Michael eyed the queen-size bed under a huge framed poster of the actress in a passionate embrace with the actor Cornel Wilde in the 1956 African adventure film *Beyond Mombasa*. "I would love to take a nap before dinner," Michael said, assuming Anthony would want to explore the neighborhood.

"That sounds great. I'm going to take a walk," he said. "This bed looks so comfortable. I might join you when I get back." Not a nap person, Michael thought Anthony must be really tired after the drive.

Anthony bought a Versace T-shirt at a boutique on West 14th Street and had made a reservation at Montrachet on West Broadway. When Anthony inquired about a dress code, the husky, inviting voice laughed. "There's no dress code, hon. Just as long as the feet and genitals are covered, it's cool." Back at the Inn, he stripped down to his Calvin's, crawled into the queen bed and spooned Michael. Michael smiled and fell back to sleep.

"239 West Broadway," Anthony told the taxi driver. Montrachet had California pinot and cabernet, Bordeaux, German Riesling, and wines from Alsace and Champagne, but most of all by far, Burgundy. This TriBeCa restaurant, named for one of the greatest and most coveted white wines in the world, initiated a new American style that combined casual dining with high-level French cooking in a desolate, barren, transitioning neighborhood.

"Damn, where the hell are we going?" Michael asked. He worried that Anthony's ignorance of Manhattan would get them killed. Looking out the cab's window, he felt they were descending into a dirty, dangerous, and destitute world. Then they arrived at 239 and the warm glow seemed like a mirage.

"Good evening, gentlemen," welcomed Walter. "Your table is ready." It felt as if they were ascending into a romantic, cozy place, far removed from the threshold they had just crossed.

For appetizers, they ordered the oyster and leek carbonara with chorizo and the Maine crab with fennel, apple, and tangerine and green peppercorn gelee. For their entrees, striped bass with green asparagus, fava beans with herb coulis and halibut en cocotte baked in a fig leaf.

When Montrachet opened, it offered a sixty bottle selection on its list, which was printed on every menu. Daniel, the restaurant's sommelier, who built the wine list into one of the greatest of the world, came to their table to answer any questions and take their wine order. "I have always been interested in trying a white Burgundy. What would you recommend?" Anthony asked.

"Well, the Puligny-Montrachet is often very mineral, with a more restrained oak character. It's a very elegant wine, less fruity. I would highly recommend it with your crab, oysters, striped bass and halibut."

For dessert, the epoisses fondue was recommended. Epoisses is a French word meaning completely worth the effort. Served with a crusty baguette, the decadent, custardy wheel was oh-so-worth-it.

"220 12th Ave and 27th Street," Anthony told the taxi driver. Looking out the cab's window, Michael felt they were descending back into that dirty, dangerous, and destitute world.

"Where the hell are we going now?" Michael asked, worrying that Anthony's ignorance of Manhattan might still get them killed, which was a real possibility on 28th Street.

The club was named for the tunnel-like shape of the main room, in which train tracks from the early 1900s ran through a sunken area of the dance floor. Anthony had never been in a space quite like it, gritty, industrial. They explored the block-long, narrow space, a dungeon like expanse of brick, granite and steel girders, catwalks, bars, a balcony, and multiple rooms on several levels. Rooms were decorated as Victorian libraries, sadomasochistic dungeons, and lounges. The bathrooms looked like locker rooms.

The Tunnel's dance floor featured several dance cages, already occupied by the Art of Seduction. They stopped at one end, looking through a fence toward an unrestored part of the building where there are still railroad tracks. "I think I just saw some rats!" Michael pointed down the dark abyss.

"This place is wild!" Anthony said, surreptitiously putting a small pill into Michael's hand. "I'll meet you back here with the rats in about one hour. I have to talk to this guy about his dancers." Michael watched as he disappeared into the crowd, off to work.

On his way to one of the lounges, Anthony stopped at a couple of cages. The go-go boys, in their black leather jock straps and boots, seduced the crowd in synchronized movements. He wanted this at Metro. In the lounge, he immediately recognized Diego from his posters and they liked each other from the start. Realizing a win-win, they agreed on four Sunday nights for the Art of Seduction.

The queasiness was beginning to dissipate, bringing on the first wave, just as he found Michael. They got a couple of waters and went up to the balcony to take in the Chelsea club scene from above, with Johnny Vicious in the booth reading the crowd. When they were told to take their shirts off during his *Ecstasy* set, it was time to dance.

Four hours later, Anthony told the taxi driver, "25 Avenue B, between East 2nd and 3rd." This time, Michael looked out the cab window, fascinated with downtown New York after-hours. Arriving at a nondescript storefront, Save the Robots was an underground club in the East Village that served only vodka, soda and juice to patrons arriving after 4 a.m. Anthony and Michael joined off-work employees of other bars and clubs, artists, musicians, drag queens and club kids on the dance floor, led by DJ Kip Lavinger, until the 8 a.m. closing.

In the blinding, early morning sunshine, Anthony told the taxi driver, "317 West 14th Street, Chelsea Pines Inn." Looking out the cab's window, Michael stroked Anthony's arm, as both were experiencing that close emotional bond enhanced by a second pill. Back with Donna Reed, the two friends cuddled and talked, kissed and talked, caressed and talked, and slept.

Promoting and waitering quickly became too much. On his last night at the Hungry I, Anthony told Richard and Stephan about the New York weekend. In an interesting twist, now they were the ones fascinated with his stories, including Daniel and the Puligny-Montrachet, Diego and his Art of Seduction, the Tunnel rats, Lady Bunny and RuPaul at Robots, and Michael at the Pines Inn with Donna Reed.

"For your next excursion, you will have to come to South Beach to visit us!" Richard said. "We just bought a house on Di Lido Island."

"Wow guys! Congratulations!"

"Move-in ready with a small guest house, too. We were thinking we will sell Louisburg Square and move there year-round."

"You won't miss the Boston Nor'easters?" Anthony said, laughing.

"Not at all," Stephan laughed, then stopped and thought, "but we will miss our friends."

Anthony arrived at Miami International and took a shuttle onto the Venetian Causeway to Di Lido Island. Richard and Stephan had been living in their gorgeous Mediterranean waterfront home now for a few months. At the front gate he is greeted with bright pink flowers of a twenty-foot tropical bougainvillea hedge and followed the tiled, palm-lined walkway to the front door. "Welcome to Miami Beach! Come on in. It's so good to see you, Anthony!" Stephan said, as they hugged. "Put your bags there for now. Let's have some coffee out at the pool and then I'll show you around later."

"That sounds great. Was an early flight and I'm working on not much sleep. Where's Richard?"

"He went to Publix to get some food for dinner tonight."

Anthony had never seen anything like this open, waterfront, outside furnished room with everything needed for entertaining, a wet bar with refrigerator, huge gas grille, custom wood cabinets and shelving, and comfortable sofas by the pool. Under the Tuscan order pillars supporting the roof, they sat sipping coffee, looking out at the

Intracoastal Waterway. Anthony asked, "So when are you getting a boat?"

"Perfect timing!" Stephan answered, as Richard joined them. "When are we getting a boat, dear?"

Anthony stood and hugged him. "You need a boat."

"We need a new kitchen, but maybe someday," he laughed. "So how was your flight?" changing the subject.

"It's always nice to be heading south the day before a blizzard!"

"We saw that on the news. The weather down here is so much healthier," Richard said. "Especially for us senior citizens."

"I hope to have half the energy you guys have at your age!"

"Talk about energy! Wait until we go out to the Warsaw Ballroom," Stephan said.

"That's what makes this a business expense."

"We knew Patrick would approve," Stephan smiled. "You look tired. I'll show you the guest house and you can settle in, relax a bit. Then we'll head to the News Café for lunch."

The corner of 8th Street and Ocean Drive was the perfect spot to people-watch. Their table at the News was going to give Anthony his first taste of SoBe. The quaint sidewalk café, newsstand and bookstore played a mix of jazz and classical music as they sipped on their Beach Babies. "Holy shit, this is delicious!" Anthony sucked up more of the pineapple, coconut and orange rum, with lemonade and orange juice in a real hand-carved coconut.

They ordered the nachos, some bruschetta, and ceviche with chips, another round of Beach Babies, and settled in for the afternoon. There was no better place to socialize than the News. Living down the street in his 19,000-square-foot villa, Versace stopped in every morning for his newspaper. Models loved the salads. Locals loved the 2-4-1 happy hour. And everyone noticed Anthony. They ordered another round with some chicken wings, conch fritters, fried mozzarella and shrimp.

"Damn, I could definitely live here," said the cruised Beach Baby.

"Nothing stopping you, is there?" said another Beach Baby, took the straw out of his mouth, "I love rum!"

"You should seriously think about it, Anthony," said the third Beach Baby. "We have the guest house," looked at his watch. "Time for happy hour!"

Club promotion on South Beach was different. Anthony still was to draw a crowd, create a safe and enjoyable atmosphere, attract a loyal following, and to make money for the club, and get paid based on a cut on the door. His contracts included coordinating and setting up special events, writing, designing, and distributing brochures and posters for those events, and maintaining an event calendar. As an independent contractor, he could do most of it in cutoffs and sometimes on rollerblades.

The next big event was the White Party fundraiser at Villa Vizcaya, a gorgeous 16th century Italian Renaissance-style villa on Biscayne Bay. James Deering, a closeted socialite, antiques collector, philanthropist, and executive at the International Harvester company, built Vizcaya between 1914 and 1922 with his "companion" Paul Chalfin.

Richard, Stephan, and Anthony sat out at the pool talking about the Network and, of course, what they were going to wear. "We were so lucky to have the Fenway Community Health Center back in Boston," Richard said. "Over the years we all used them for our unique health needs."

"True. South Florida had to quickly build a support network, and thanks to the grassroots efforts of Frank Wager and Jorge Suarez and those first 1,600 white-wearing partiers, the Health Crisis Network got up and running," Stephan said.

"Speaking of white-wearing, we need to look fabulous!" Richard reminded them. "Let's go shopping on Lincoln Road later."

And on that Thanksgiving weekend, they did look fabulous, as did the five hundred others disembarking at the Vizcaya dock. They joined the thousands of other guests dressed as all-white cowboys, Indians, clowns, dancers, swans, unicorns, angels, devils, divas, or sailors. While the costumes were truly amazing, each individual white outfit formed an army of white knights on a noble quest to help the world eliminate the pain and suffering caused by HIV/AIDS. That weekend, Anthony decided he would use his experience with boats and promotion to join the fight, in Dan's memory.

Anthony was gliding down Ocean Drive on his roller blades, promoting his first white party boat cruise to benefit the Health Crisis Network. He noticed this really handsome guy walking Ocean Drive in his jacket and tie. He approached Anthony as he was securing the boat cruise information onto a light pole. "You move pretty well on those!" he looked down at Anthony's legs. "I'm Carlos."

"Thanks, great to meet you, Carlos. I'm Anthony." They shook hands. "Yeah, I have to cover Washington, Collins, and Lincoln before I work the beach."

"I work for the Convention and Visitors Bureau. Carlos looked more closely at the poster. "Wow, you got David to DJ. I think I better buy a ticket before you sell out."

Anthony reached into his shorts and gave Carlos the tickets, telling him not to worry about it.

"Thanks, give me a few of those posters. I'll help you out."

"See you in white next week!" As they hugged, "by the way, you need anything?"

"Sure, maybe two?" Anthony knew then they would be friends.

Anthony hired two of Diego's dancers to decorate and help with set-up. The two level, 74-foot party yacht was awash in white balloons and bunting. He welcomed the one hundred twenty guests arriving at the dockyard pier for the sunset launch, collecting tickets at embarkation, while David's pre-cruise rhythms navigated the white-clad partiers onto the open deck or down into the lower level bar and dance floor.

David began the night with *The Whistle Song*'s flute, amplified as it traveled over the calm bay water, sending a message out in all directions that this was the Beach event for the next four hours. Time for a break, Anthony joined Carlos at the bar. "Congratulations Anthony! People will be talking about this tomorrow!" Carlos said. The two friends stood together, taking it all in.

"Dan would have loved this."

The captain maneuvered the boat so the crew could secure the lines and ready the gangplank for disembarkation. The passengers would transition from floating to the more familiar grounded Warsaw.

Carlos passed Anthony the keys. He started the ignition, popped a pill in his mouth and finished off his bottle of water. "So, did you make any money?" Carlos asked.

"I did, but not sure how much yet." He asked Carlos to help him figure it out.

Anthony found a parking spot. They said hi to Jaime at the red velvet rope, and moved into position at their corner of the bar. "I've gotta get Michael down here," he said to Carlos. "Can't wait for you to meet him."

"Yeah, you talk about him all the time! I feel like I already have."

"Well, I found a place of my own on Meridian. Good size 2-bedroom for half the rent in Boston. Moving there next week."

"Nice! It will be so much easier for you to be on the beach here."

"I know. I'll miss Richard and Stephan, but the bike ride from their place sucks. Once I settle into the new place I'll invite Michael to stay with me a while. He has some new accounts in Miami."

The bartender put out two waters for them. Anthony looked out at the Warsaw revelers, many in white, and felt a pride from what he had accomplished that night. He also felt a rush from the X he took earlier that night. David brought in DJ

Eddie X from LA. The underground deep House of his *Fastlane* mix from L.E.X. Sound Factory, featuring Jemeni and Jelleestone, got them out under the laser fan. Eddie's entire life was about movement. He began his career in entertainment as a dancer, studying at the Alvin Allie and Martha Graham Schools, and choreographed for Black Box and C&C Music Factory. Anthony and Carlos danced until the house lights announced it was time for Mac's Club Deuce.

The white-and-pastel-blue Deco beauty on the corner of Meridian and 16th would be home for a while. The courtyard fountain's impatiens were beginning to wilt in the early summer heat. Moving into the second floor apartment, Anthony and Carlos felt the same. A cool shower in the bathroom with the porthole window would finish the relocation. A batch of iced Margaritas would begin the revivification. "You make a mean Margarita my friend!" Carlos said.

"Plenty of practice at the pirate parties."

"So when is Michael arriving?"

"Tomorrow morning. I'll bring him to the beach in the afternoon to meet everyone."

"Great! I'll see what's happening tomorrow night, Carlos said. "Maybe Bobby's Hombre, or Garage at the Institute, Fetish at the Cameo,

Bend...Over at Boomerang, AM/PM, Trouble at Art/Act, or a barbeque at Torpedo."

"We'll give him a good taste of South Beach on his first day. And then Warsaw on Wednesday!"

Anthony spent the first night in his new apartment emptying kitchen boxes, putting clothes away in his bedroom, towels in the bathrooms, and making the beds. He knew Michael would love his room, except for the Harley's running down 16th to Ocean Drive. It was a noisy intersection.

As the taxi drove away, Anthony gave Michael a hug and helped him with his luggage up the stairs. "Here's your room," he said. "Why don't you get out of those jeans and into some shorts? I'll make us some coffee."

They sat chatting a while in the kitchen. Anthony wanted to catch up on any Boston news, but he couldn't wait to take Michael for a walk to the beach. Looking at his shorts though, he needed to take him to a newly opened, gay-owned shop on 13th. Michael bought some new shorts, a couple of square cut swim trunks and some sleeveless tees.

On their way to the beach they stopped to get a shot of wheatgrass juice. "This is a powerful detoxifier," Anthony said. "I stop here every day." Michael had never heard of it, but had a feeling he would be drinking it regularly.

When Anthony found his group of friends, they began introductions. Carlos got up, hugged Michael and stood next to Anthony. "Come on Michael, let's get you wet." Waist deep and always cruising, "So what are we doing tonight?" Anthony asked Carlos.

"Public opening at Bobby's Hombre tonight. I've heard Versace will be there. The Del Rubio Triplets are performing. Should be a great introduction to South Beach for Michael," Carlos laughed.

Anthony and Michael went back to the apartment to shower. "You rest up for tonight, Michael," Anthony said. "I have to meet Sarah before dinner. I'll be back around six." He had a feeling he knew who Sarah was.

Anthony would see most of his customers at Hombre. His increasing supply needed to cover the Wednesday and Saturday nights' Warsaw demand. He met Sarah at a small party that Richard and Stephan brought him to on Collins Ave when he first moved from Boston, and they hit if off right away. A fiery Corsican redhead, she actually didn't mind being called a fag hag. "You have the most beautiful hair!" Anthony told her.

"Why thank you," she smiled, playing with it in her fingers. "My grandmother, from Corsica, had the same color. She used to tell me that a person had to spit on the road after a redhead walked past to ward off evil spirits. Some people thought they were related to Satan!"

"Many redheads were thought to be witches and burnt at the stake," Richard added. "Then morph into the undead and become vampires!" They all looked at Sarah, and wondered.

Sarah ran ecstasy for her distributor for a few hundred dollars a week. MDMA often came into Florida from Europe, especially the Netherlands and Belgium by way of Israeli and Russian drug smuggling rings. Caribbean, Colombian and Dominican drug rings also brought E into Florida, but she wasn't interested in those contacts, or that business.

She made most of her cash doing deals of her own with customers in Miami-Dade, who would buy mainly for personal consumption. She got about an ounce at a time that can make a large sandwich bag of three hundred pills. Always precise with her math, she would mark up the drug between two and three times what she bought it for when selling it to her customers, of which Anthony became one the night of that party.

The next day, while Michael was out riding his new bike, Anthony did his rounds. He didn't want customers coming to his apartment, and he never wanted to have too much on him at Warsaw. In Florida, the penalties for possession of less than ten grams of MDMA can include five years in prison, a $5,000 fine, vehicle forfeiture and driver's license suspension. Possession of ten grams or more is felony drug trafficking and comes with a minimum three year sentence. With the typical ecstasy dose being 100 milligrams, it would take one hundred capsules or more to reach the threshold of trafficking.

After a lunch break at the News with Michael and Carlos, Anthony continued promoting and distributing for that night. As he worked the afternoon, he thought about how he wanted Michael's first night at Warsaw to be indelible, from the cafecitos, Jaime's greeting, the corner-bar rendezvous, David's house trance, Diego's Seduction, and the induced euphoria.

That night, with their brains loaded with serotonin and dopamine, David used the British acid house of M|A|R|R|S to *Pump Up the Volume,* and the Machine ordered the sea of Ballroom bonding to dance, dance! Michael looked over at Anthony and Carlos and smiled, looked up at the blue lasers and smiled, looked beyond at David and smiled. Michael's first night at Warsaw would certainly be indelible.

Anthony and Michael settled into their daily routines on the Beach. For Anthony, that included his promoting and morning workouts at Jeramiah's. Monday was legs and abs, with some cardio. Tuesday was chest and triceps. Wednesday was cardio. Thursday was back, biceps and abs. Friday was shoulders, calves and forearms, with some cardio. Saturday and Sunday were much needed recovery days. For Michael, his routine included push-ups and bike rides and the occasional sales meeting. Once in a while he would have to return to Boston for a face-to-face, but the remote support he provided was usually enough.

And of course, it was all about the beach. The socializing, sunbathing, swimming, volleyball, and people-watching on the white sand, in the warm crystal-clear water, on Ocean Drive from 5th to 15th. Anthony wouldn't be here if not for the beach, and neither would the Art Deco hotels, restaurants, clubs, and bars. So daily he would join the locals, tourists, and friends on that white sandy beach. And every night he would join those same locals, tourists, and friends at those clubs and bars. But there was one club that all those locals, tourists, and friends talked about on the beach. And there was an approaching event at that club that didn't seem to require much promotion.

The Warsaw Second Anniversary Party would transcend the usual South Beach debauchery. Anthony had heard about a few things that might get the Miami Beach Police involved. Those rumors explained the line down Española Way. Jaime was remunerated with a small ziploc bag as he released the hook from the stanchion. Jacqueline then collected her thirty dollars, as debauchery didn't come cheap.

Anthony, Carlos, and Michael would begin their five hour bacchanalia together, as three ice-cold waters were served on the bar. Just as Anthony felt that first roll, David began the Party in total darkness, with the command to dance now! That darkness gave the Art of Seduction cover to take their places. In a burst of white light and tribal rap, the Warsaw then decreed that everyone was to dance until they couldn't dance no more.

Anthony had no idea who the final ziploc bags were for, but they needed to take a walk. He took Michael's hand and began shoving his way through any unfamiliar group, passing by the occupied penis, and two of Diego's work-booted dancers, to the VIP stairs. Marcos received the obligatory hugs and kisses, whispered something to Anthony and small packets were transferred. Someone upstairs trusted Marcos. Anthony felt relieved, his work done, it was time for pill number two, and to escape to the dance floor.

He washed down the pill and felt warm and cold from the sweat, with Michael and Carlos, alone together, and hundreds of others. Rolls accompanied the laser lights with surreal sideshow performances, freakish, dreamlike. Pulsing, tribal, techno-electronic house beats forced compliance of the earlier dance command until The Bear is aglow in white light.

Anthony thought of Dan as she sang Gloria Gaynor's *I Will Survive*. The house lights come on to a round of applause, not just for The Bear, but for the Warsaw. Outside, old and new friends decide how they will spend the early morning. "Let's close the Deuce," Carlos broadcasts, as these three friends head down 14th Street.

To the Looking-Glass world it was Alice that said
"I've a sceptre in hand, I've a crown on my head.
Let the Looking-Glass creatures, whatever they be

Come dine with the Red Queen,
the White Queen
and Me!"

Lewis Carroll

CARLOS

Carlos removed his grip on the White Knight and shouts "Check!" His mom moves her index finger up to her mouth for the familiar signal that he was too loud. His arms, as if conducting a crazed orchestra, not able to contain the excitement, tell what his mom already knows. He has won another game.

"There's no use trying," she said. "One can't believe impossible things."

The seven-year old completes the *Through the Looking Glass* quote. "I daresay you haven't had much practice. When I was your age, I always did it for half-an-hour a day. Why, sometimes I've believed as many as six impossible things before breakfast."

Nalda quietly studied the board, looked up at her son, and smiled. "I think it's checkmate!" and she gently laid her king on its side. "Good game, Carlos!" She reached over and shook his hand.

"Thanks mom!"

She was always told as a child that her name meant...strong. As a young mother, she has proven herself to be just that. Winning in chess was not the only goal for Carlos. Looking her in the eyes, saying thank you and shaking her hand was just as important. Persistence takes strength. Knowledge takes strength. Optimism takes strength. There are days she wondered what were her parents thinking when they named her Nalda.

Getting Carlos the services he needed in school was a constant battle. Knowing the latest research, strategies, and jargon meant hours in the library and seeking the advice of other parents with similar experiences. But Nalda always knew Carlos would do just fine in life.

Kitty is a Boston Terrier. Kitty is highly intelligent, easily trained, but can be stubborn at times. Kitty is Carlos's best friend, actually his only friend. When Nalda brought the Boston home, Carlos announced his name, "Kitty!"

"No, he's not a cat, he's a dog!"

"I know he's a dog, mom."

Relieved, she agreed to the name.

Carlos often related daily events to *Through the Looking Glass*. So it was no surprise when he said, "Kitty, can you play chess? Now, don't smile, my dear, I'm asking it seriously. Because, when we were playing just now, you watched just as if you understood it, and when I said 'Check!' you purred!"

Kitty is prone to snorting and gagging sounds because Bostons have tiny nostrils and narrow trachea. Carlos calls these Kitty sounds purring, although it's more of a grunt. It makes Carlos laugh appropriately, which is unusual. Sometimes he calls the sound outgribing. When Alice asks Humpty Dumpty "And what does 'outgrabe' mean?" Carlos, in his best Humpty, will say "Well, 'outgribing' is something between bellowing and whistling, with a kind of sneeze in the middle. However, you'll hear it done...and when you've heard it you'll be quite content."

Carlos will often explain the hard words in Jabberwocky to his mom. She pretends she understands, or even cares, because it's a window into his mind. Each time she rereads the Humpty Dumpty chapter, she gets more confused. Yet, at this time in his life, it is his world. And she will try to meet him there.

But maybe she is Humpty Dumpty trying to explain a world to Carlos that he doesn't understand, or worse, scares him. She wants him to go out into the world destroying his fears. She wants her son not to lose his curiosity, and be brave. But he is afraid of some touch, some sound, some smell, some taste, and some sight.

Carlos really doesn't like to be touched. By anything, or anyone. He doesn't mind being the one touching, just don't touch him.

Carlos can be rendered helpless by sound. Loud noises and crowded places make him feel sick, or so he says.

Carlos is a very picky eater, so he doesn't like most smells coming from the kitchen before dinner. It makes him feel sick, or so he says.

Carlos doesn't like the taste of most foods. But the way he describes the food he doesn't like is by the way it feels or sounds in his mouth.

Carlos doesn't like bright light, flashing light, and florescent light, especially florescent light. He says it's too loud.

"Carlos, finish your breakfast. You are going to miss the bus again!"

Mom knew I didn't like runny eggs. And now the yellowy-orange was running onto my toast and bacon. I like toast and bacon, but I don't like my food touching. And I really don't like runny eggs. "I can't eat this now, mom."

"Fine, take an apple. I am not driving you to school today."

The bus is always so loud. My school gave me some headphones that blocked the yelling. I put an apple in my backpack where my headphones are. I allowed mom to kiss me on my forehead, no hugs. I hugged Kitty.

I was glad I didn't need a coat. I don't like coats. I should be on a special bus, but my mom wants me on the regular yellow bus. It was 2 minutes late. I always sit in the seat behind Mr. O'Neil. Just in case. He smells like Old Spice. We are supposed to arrive at school at 8:10 am. The 24 hours of the day are divided into a.m. from the Latin ante meridiem, meaning "before midday", and p.m. from the Latin post meridiem meaning "after midday". Mr. O'Neil would have to drive faster to make up for the 2 minutes. He never went over the speed limit of 30 miles per hour. We got to school at 8:16 am. The first bell rings at 8:30 am. I keep my headphones on until after the bell.

I am in the fourth grade, but I don't go to a fourth grade classroom. I go to a special room, where I look at pictures of people's faces and I practice the right responses when people ask me questions. My favorite subject is Math. I like numbers. My least favorite subject is recess. I always get in trouble during recess. Mom calls it "having a fit." Sometimes I hit kids if they make fun of me, and back in the classroom we talk about controlling my anger.

Middle school sucked.

I didn't have to go to a special classroom in high school. My favorite subject was still Math. My Algebra teacher also did chess club after school. Mr. Hughes was cool, he understood me. And I started to make some friends. We talked about Star Wars, chess, cars and college. They talked about girls, a lot. I thought about Harrison Ford, a lot. Why did I always have to be so different from the rest? I knew I could never talk about being gay or *Through the Looking Glass* with my friends.

"So, how was your day today, buddy?" Mr. Hughes would always ask, as we set up the chess pieces. And he really wanted to know. Mom always asked too. So did Kitty. No one else really wanted to know.

"I got my acceptance letter from BU yesterday, so today has been a pretty good day."

"Wow! Congratulations Carlos," he reached over the chess board to shake my hand. I was anticipating a hand shake, so it was OK. Especially from Mr. Hughes. I knew he would be excited because Boston University was where he got his degree in teaching. "So what does mom think about you moving away from Miami?"

"Well, we have always known I had to go away to college, to see if I can do life on my own."

The Supported Education Services program at BU helped Carlos adapt to college life and motivated him to seek out the Boston social scene. The urban campus is situated in the Kenmore and Fenway neighborhoods along the Charles River. BU students had many bar options surrounding Fenway Park, some gay, some straight, some mixed.

Carlos became a regular at the 1270. Known as the 12, he often sat on the first floor bleachers next to a bongo player, accompanying Elvis Costello or Annie Lennox. The upstairs dance floor was disco. Too much sensory overload, Carlos often escaped to the rooftop bar for a burger, and good conversation, sometimes to the background muffled cheers from Red Sox fans.

Looking out at the Fenway lights, behind left field, Carlos thought about the upcoming Sunday night at the Metro on Lansdowne Street. Built as a garage for the Boston Globe delivery horses, carriages and trucks, it became a venue for Dylan, The Who, Led Zeppelin and Dead concerts. The disco era brought multiple renovations, from 12 Lansdowne to Boston-Boston and Metro. Sunday was always gay night, bringing out a capacity crowd.

Instead of living in a dorm, Carlos had a studio apartment in an old rooming house. Jason lived in the same building. Also a BU student, they were becoming good friends, and he was able to talk Carlos into finally going out to the Metro. "My friend is getting a delivery from New York," Jason said, taking another bite of his burger. "I'll go over there before we head out Sunday."

They met at Jason's apartment. Instead of beers, he poured two glasses of water with lemon wedges. He then handed Carlos a small Ziploc bag. Each package contained before, during and after directions, and a white pill. "We should start to feel the X kick in about thirty minutes after we get to Metro. If your stomach starts to feel weird, don't worry, it doesn't last long. About an hour later, you'll peek for a few hours." He swallows the pill and drinks some water.

110

Carlos takes the pill in his thumb and forefinger, "You promise to stay with me tonight?"

"Of course! We'll do whatever you want to do," Jason assured him.

He placed the pill on his tongue and washed it down. Boston is a great walking city, but Jason thought it might be better to take a taxi. Rain was forecast. "We don't want to get to the club soaking wet, and there might be a line."

They arrived before the line and the cover. Jason wanted Carlos to familiarize himself with the massive, open space. XTC could be disorienting, so they walked over to the bar on the right side of the dance floor, running its length. "If we get separated, this is our meeting spot, OK?" The bartender came over to them and Jason ordered two waters.

Relieved that his friend would think of that, "OK, good idea," he said, looking around, taking it all in. He had never been in a club as expansive as Metro. There was a twin bar on the other side of the dance floor. The lighting and sound system was as technically advanced as any in the country. A stage was on the far side, with the two-floor punk club behind it, called Spit, open to Metro patrons on Sunday nights. Jason thought it would be better if they stayed on the Metro side tonight. "I'm feeling kinda queasy," Carlos said. "Can we go sit a while?"

111

"Sure, let's go over to the booths. Great spot to watch the place come to life." Carlos had noticed that the dance floor was pretty empty, but there was a steady stream of people passing by them as they settled into a half circle wall bench to watch the show about to begin.

"Holy shit!" Carlos said, looking around the club. "Everything looks clearer. It's like I got new contact lenses!"

"Yeah, you're starting to feel it," Jason smiled. "Let me know when you feel like dancing."

The lighting platforms slowly descended from the ceiling. Once in place, the transformation was instantaneous. Blue laser accompanied the live piano introduction of Marshall Jefferson's *Move Your Body*. The crowd obeyed. Punched in their chests by the powerful base line, Jason can't wait any longer and takes Carlos by the hand. Enveloped by the touch of light and sound, Carlos, for the first time in his life, desired physical sensation. The serendipity of Curtis McClain's "sexy body" observation fused the two friends, shirtless, for the duration.

Jason knew they needed to break from the hypnotic state of the dancefloor. He gave Carlos a long, deep kiss and said, "Take my hand. We need some water." Surprised their booth remained unoccupied, "I'll be right back, don't go anywhere." After what seemed like forever, he returned with the waters and some limes. "Just sip the water, don't drink too much. Here, try sucking on a lime, it can be pretty intense!"

Never one for intensity in his mouth, the melding of the lime scent along with the tangy sweetness of the juice was intoxicating, exhilarating. The smell of a clove cigarette wafted through the air, carried by the coolness of dance floor fog. He gently caresses the crevice between Jason's abs as Jason massages his arm. Carlos notices the interest in the faces as they pass by. "I think they like what they see," running his hand over Jason's cheek and through his hair.

"What's not to like?" smiling and pinching his nipple. Carlos pulls back, laughing. Jason takes his hand, "Let's get back out there!"

Capacity is one thousand five hundred. Instead of panic, Carlos is overwhelmed with joy. An empathy he didn't think was possible. Perhaps even love. He feels alone with Jason on the packed dancefloor under the most intense white light, peaking with Dr. Alban, *Sing Hallelujah!* The house lights snap out. In disorientating total darkness, Soul II Soul sings *Back to Life*, a cappella, in the style of the chapel, as the lights gradually fade up. Jason signals it's time for more water, so they work their way to the bar.

"We should leave before last call so we can get a taxi. Lansdowne gets crazy at closing, especially when it's raining. How you doing?"

"Never been better! I'm ready when you are."

Jason put on some music, lit a few candles, and filled the deep clawfoot tub with warm water. "I think you're going to enjoy this." He added some Dead Sea bath salt with eucalyptus oil and swooshed it around. Carlos wondered if the two of them would fit comfortably. They did.

As they dried off, Carlos felt both relaxed from the warmth of the water and invigorated from the coolness of the eucalyptus. Jason had thought of everything, even clean sheets. They held each other and talked. They caressed each other and talked. They talked until sunrise. And then they slept. They were not going to classes today. That was for damn sure.

Carlos was looking forward to telling Susan all about his night out at Metro. She was his counselor at SES, and he had lots of questions. It had been a week, and he was sure she would have lots of questions, too. She always started with "So how you doing Carlos? How's your day been?" Just like Mr. Hughes, only Susan didn't play chess. He told her about Jason, taking X, Metro, the music, the dancing, the lights, the tub, the caressing, and the sunrise.

And then he said, "Susan, I feel different."

"What do you mean by different?"

"I feel a part of the world now. I'm not afraid. Don't get me wrong, I'm still confused, just not afraid. It's hard to describe."

"Do you mind me asking, do you think the ecstasy had something to do with this change?"

"I've thought a lot about that this week, and I do. I need to understand why."

"Good. I think I can help. I know the Lead Clinical Research Associate at MAPS, the Multidisciplinary Association for Psychedelic Studies. They are researching the psychiatric benefits of MDMA or ecstasy on people with autism. Would you like to talk to her about your experience?"

"Sure, I'd like that."

"Here's her card. Give her a call to set up an appointment, and I'll see you next week. But before you go, Carlos, be very careful with this new experience. Self-medicating is not smart."

"Thanks Susan. I understand. This should be interesting." They hugged longer than usual, and Carlos didn't mind.

Carlos returned to Miami with a BA in economics and mathematics and a minor in hospitality management. He also returned to Miami as a confident young man, hoping for the best, prepared for the worst. His mom had cancer.

Nalda loved her Marlboro Menthols. She started smoking the smooth tasting, minty cigarette as a teenager. Induced by conformity, maintained by stress relief, and uninfluenced by the warnings, the lit cigarette was as much a part of her day as the cups of coffee.

At first, she thought the cough and difficulty breathing were the remnants of a nasty cold. She thought the increasing fatigue was due to working two jobs. And she wasn't all that disappointed with the weight loss, at first.

The diagnosis was extensive-stage small-cell lung carcinoma. The prognosis was grim. Persistence, knowledge and optimism weren't going to be enough this time, but she did have the strength to travel to Boston and see Carlos graduate.

She wanted to be at home, in control of her own destiny. He wanted her to leave peacefully, with the dignity she deserved.

"I hope you know how proud I am of you," she told him, "and my love and strength will be with you when I'm gone."

Holding her hand, Carlos reached over to kiss her. "I am forever grateful for what you have done for me. I love you, mom." He put on Simon and Garfunkel's *Sounds of Silence*, as planned, and went for a walk. And when he returned, she was gone, as planned. He held her hand, and reached over and kissed her.

As in life, so in death, Nalda took good care of her son. He had no school debt, was able to buy a condo on Miami Beach, and a car. But he wanted a job. The Greater Miami Convention & Visitors Bureau was looking for a Partner Representative. Without any sales experience, nevertheless, he was hired. Sometimes it helps to be tall, dark and handsome. He had his mom to thank for teaching him how to work that.

Carlos became the Bureau's first liaison to the LGBT and LGBT-friendly business community in Miami Beach. New hospitality, culinary and retail businesses were opening in SoBe along with the influx of gay and lesbian residents and tourists. His role was to promote networking within the community as well as to promote the Beach as a year-round gay-friendly tourist destination. So it was inevitable that he would cross paths with Anthony.

Anthony was gliding down Ocean Drive on his roller blades, promoting a white party boat cruise. Carlos was walking Ocean Drive in his jacket and tie, distributing the Visitors Bureau monthly magazine. Neither one known to miss out on an opportunity, business or personal, Carlos approached Anthony as he was securing the event information onto a light pole. "You move pretty well on those!" looking down at Anthony's legs. "I'm Carlos."

"Thanks, great to meet you, Carlos. I'm Anthony." They shook hands. "Yeah, I have to cover Washington, Collins, and Lincoln before I work the beach. I'd ask you to join me but you're not exactly dressed for it."

He grabbed his tie, "I hate this." He studied the poster. "Wow, you got David to DJ. I think I better buy a ticket before you sell out."

"Oh no, I'll comp you. Here's two," Anthony reached into his shorts and gave Carlos the tickets.

"See you in white next week!" As they hugged, "by the way, you need anything?"

"Sure, maybe two?" And that began a lasting friendship.

The two level, 74-foot party yacht was already decorated in white balloons. The theme became more evident as Anthony and David welcomed the one hundred twenty guests arriving at the dockyard pier for a sunset launch. Anthony collected tickets at embarkation, while David's pre-cruise distinct piano and cymbal rhythms sent that theme out to the parking lot, navigating the white-clad partiers onto the open deck or down into the lower level bar and dance floor.

A white limousine drove up to the pier. Carlos watched as the driver opened the door and

Jacqueline stepped out in a stunning white Versace dress. Xavier took her arm and two of Diego's dancers escorted them onto the boat, hopping up onto their deck platforms for the evening, they never missed a beat. "Miss Jackie, you look gorgeous!" Carlos announced. He took her raised hand and turned her around gracefully. She appreciated the opportunity to display her hard work to the deck audience.

One long, prolonged blast of the boat's horn signaled an ear-splitting departure and some stealth pill swallowing. "Welcome aboard everyone," the captain announced. "Please listen carefully to the following important safety information." Carlos heard something about lifejackets and abandoning ship. "We will be heading to the tip of Miami Beach through Government Cut," the captain continued, "returning to Biscayne Bay for the duration of the cruise. Enjoy the sunset over Downtown and have a fun evening!"

David began the night with *The Whistle Song*'s flute, amplified as it traveled over the calm bay water, sending a message out in all directions that this was the Beach event for the next four hours. Time for a break, Anthony joined Carlos at the bar. "Congratulations, people will be talking about this tomorrow!" Carlos said. The two friends stood together, taking it all in.

Looking out at the dancefloor, white fabric was beginning to transition into various shades of tanned skin. Looking out the port windows, sunset orange was transitioning into midnight blue. And Carlos began that anticipated transition from queasiness to euphoria. Dancing while floating, and rolling with water breaks out on the upper deck, he was surprised to hear Gloria Gaynor's voice so soon. The captain maneuvered the boat so the crew could secure the lines and ready the gangplank for disembarkation. The passengers would transition from floating to the more familiar grounded Warsaw.

Carlos waited for Anthony to take care of the final cruise business. "You have to drive," Carlos said the obvious, passing him the keys. Anthony had some catching up to do. He started the ignition, popped a pill in his mouth and finished off his bottle of water. "So, did you make any money?" Carlos asked.

"I did, but not sure how much yet. Maybe you can help me tomorrow figure out exactly how much?"

"Sure, your miscellaneous expenses might be a little out of control!"

"Yeah, maybe. Cost of doing business on South Beach." They both nodded as Anthony found a parking spot. They said hi to Jaime, and moved into position at their corner of the bar. David brought in DJ Eddie X from LA. He knew many in white would arrive already well into their roll, and had to meet them there. Known for his throbbing underground deep house and tribal sound, he would not disappoint.

When Carlos had a day off, he was at the 12th Street Beach on Lummus Park. The wide strip of sand, much of it imported from the Bahamas, stretches from South Pointe at the end of Miami Beach to the giant hotels thirty blocks to the north. But 12th Street Beach is loudly and proudly gay, as the rainbow flags by the lifeguard stations announce. There are some pockets of lesbians, and even a few straight women, who enjoy bathing topless away from prying eyes of straight men, but this was where Carlos and his friends went to gossip and people-watch after a morning at the gym.

Anthony found them settled on the towels and began introductions. "We've heard a lot about you Michael. It's great finally meeting you. How long are you here for?" Carlos got up, hugged Michael and stood next to Anthony.

"At least the month, maybe more depending on work."

"So what are we doing tonight?" Anthony asked Carlos.

"Public opening at Hombre tonight down on 6th." That night Carlos introduced Michael to

Versace and the Del Rubio triplets. It was his South Beach inauguration. A few days later, they would introduce him to Warsaw. Carlos was impressed.

Carlos liked making fashion statements, and the Anniversary Party would certainly be a night for one. It was time to dye the white jeans, and lemon zest would be the statement.

He got paper towels handy and put on his rubber gloves, and filled a plastic container with three gallons of hot water. To enhance the color, he added one cup of salt and one teaspoon of dish detergent to help promote level dyeing. To achieve the darkest yellow possible, he added the whole bottle of Rit to the dye bath. He wet the jeans and added them to the dyebath, stirring slowly and continuously. Carlos knew the first ten minutes are the most critical. Stirring helps to ensure an even color with no splotches. He watched until the desired lemon zest was achieved and remove them from the dyebath. He knew they would look darker when wet. He squeezed out the excess dye and rinsed them in cool water until the rinse water ran clear. Finally, he washed them in warm water, rinsed, and dried his new jeans.

Anthony invited him over for pasta, so he would have to move his ass. A short enough walk from Collins to Meridian, but his antiperspirant would fail him. The air conditioning felt fabulous and the sauce smelled fabulous. He always looked forward to Anthony's meatballs. He looked forward to a strong, sweet shot of cafecito, too.

From Washington to Collins, seeing the line signaled an event beyond ordinary. Jaime would have to deal with some queens with attitude. It was early, yet everyone paid cover tonight, and Jacqueline would have no problem dealing with those queens! Settled into their corner, Carlos noticed the ten-foot penis at the other end of the bar. He thought once the XTC kicked in, it was going to be an interesting night.

He watched the enormous woman being helped onto the penis by Tomas and Joshua. He had met Nelson one night while he was sitting on the bar, but Carlos had no idea who the woman was. He needed to find out. Nelson crawled down off the thigh, which was bigger than him, to say hello to Carlos. All he could think about was Alice finding the little bottle with the words "Drink me" printed on the label. "Hi Nelson," he reached out to shake his hand. "Well, look at you!"

"Hi Carlos," Nelson spun around. "You like the costume?" He loved masks.

"I do!" he said, a bit confused.

"This is Judy. She performs at Magnum. Judy meet Carlos."

"Nice to meet you, Carlos," she said, projecting her voice from above.

"She's also known as The Bear in Key West and Provincetown."

"Oh? I'll have to ask my friends if they have seen you." Distracted by Madonna's *Justify* and the silhouetted ballet dancers up on the catwalk, he waved bye and headed back to join Anthony and Michael.

Carlos was on the cusp of moving from the main beat to the cross-beats, to that XTC state of consciousness with his friends. They ground him, just as with Jason the first time. Instead of that long-past social panic, he is overwhelmed with joy and empathy and love. A lasting awareness and acceptance of himself.

Carlos watches as Jacqueline and Diego take their places, surreptitiously orchestrating the end of the Anniversary celebration. The E7 arpeggio chord is rolled up the piano and back down again, David's signature last song. A floodlight hits The Bear, and Carlos knows this will be a special moment in South Beach history. That message of personal strength and defiance, from which fear turns into a resolution of survival, and love. The house lights come on to a round of applause. Heading toward the door, he asks Jacqueline and Xavier, "See you at the Deuce?"

"Oh yes! We will be there soon. I need to introduce Judy to someone first and get into some comfortable shoes."

A Wasp in a Wig

"When I was young, my ringlets waved
And curled and crinkled on my head:
And then they said 'You should be shaved,
And wear a yellow wig instead.'
But when I followed their advice,
And they had noticed the effect,
They said I did not look so nice
As they had ventured to expect.
They said it did not fit, and so
It made me look extremely plain:
But what was I to do, you know?
My ringlets would not grow again.
So now that I am old and grey,
And all my hair is nearly gone,
They take my wig from me and say
'How can you put such rubbish on?'
And still, whenever I appear,
They hoot at me and call me 'Pig!'
And that is why they do it, dear,
Because I wear a yellow wig."

Lewis Carroll

JACQUELINE

Jack attended Saint Peter Elementary School in South Boston. His curiosity and constant questioning were not exactly encouraged or rewarded by the Poor Sisters of Jesus Crucified and the Sorrowful Mother. He quickly learned to keep certain thoughts to himself. However, he fondly remembers the librarian, Sister Caterina.

She took the name of Sister Caterina de Erazu. Caterina fled her Spanish convent dressed as a man in the 17th century. Traveling through Spain, Peru, Chile and Mexico as a sword master, mule-driver and soldier, she avoided execution by claiming she was a virgin and a nun. The pope pardoned her and permitted her to wear men's clothes for the rest of her life. She fell in love with the wife of a hidalgo and died following a duel with him.

Sister Caterina noticed that Jack was having trouble finding a book. "Jack, do you know the author Lewis Carroll?"

"No Sister, I don't think so."

"Well, let's go find one of his books. I think you might enjoy his stories." They walked over to the C's and found Carroll. She picked two red bound books from the shelf and handed them to him. "I hope you enjoy these books Jack, and I want you to keep them as a gift from me, OK?"

"Yes Sister, thank you. I will start reading one when I get home. Thank you!" No one had ever given Jack a book before. He saw a white rabbit holding a pocket watch on one cover. He opened to the first page and he read *Alice's Adventures in Wonderland*. The second book had a frog on the cover and inside he read *Through the Looking-Glass, And What Alice Found There*.

Although certainly working class, Jack didn't have much in common with his Irish Catholic classmates. Southie is home to some of the oldest and toughest public housing projects in the United States. With a Jewish father and Italian mother, growing up on D Street would have been difficult enough, but Jack loved to wear his mother's clothes.

After Saint Peter's, Jack attended Southie High. Every day that he got home without getting punched either in the face or stomach or both was a good day, and one day closer to graduation. "What do you expect having mixed parents?" his grandmother would say, blaming his dad. He thought she was such a fucking ignorant bitch! The boys punching him could give a shit about the Jewishness. It was all about the rumored dresses.

One of his uncles owned the neighborhood gym. Jack had never been in there, but enough was enough. It was time for some life lessons in self-defense. Turns out that being light on his feet was good for dancing, and boxing! Using proper footwork is an important component to punching power. On one of those walks home from school, that power was generated from his ankles to the knees, to the thighs to his core, to the chest, to the shoulders, to the forearms, to his fist and finally into Shawn O'Sullivan's face. Semi-conscious on the ground, Shawn learned an important life lesson that day. Never mess with a drag queen.

Jack needed to escape his South Boston neighborhood, so he moved to Miami Beach, where his other uncle owned a popular Italian restaurant. Jacqueline worked there for many years and learned to make the delicious dishes close friends were always lucky enough to experience. Gianni Versace loved her lasagna. In drag since 1958, Jacqueline certainly earned the title Queen of South Beach.

Jacqueline is a survivor. During the 1950s, city and state government worked to shut down gay bars and enacted laws making homosexuality and cross-dressing illegal. Selling alcohol to homosexuals was illegal. Her uncle's mob connections, in the day, allowed for safe, regular police escorts home after a bar raid.

Sometimes those connections weren't enough. Jacqueline once got arrested for wearing women's clothes. She had bought some ruffled shirts and hip huggers from a men's store called Slack Shack on Lincoln Road, but the judge dismissed the case when she showed him the receipt.

A few months later, she was called to jury duty and wanted to look her best. Wearing her expensive white fox and period girdle, she couldn't pass through the metal detector. She assumed it was the metal forms and lifted her dress to show the security guard. Gaining the attention of the gentlemen around her, the guard told her to lower her dress. Once inside, when the court official called for Jack, and Jacqueline stood up, she was summarily dismissed.

It takes skill and a lot of makeup to transition into a lady with class. Unlike many of her contemporaries, a woman of a certain age must be dignified as well as glamorous. Not many have seen Jack. Beginning with a good moisturizing, followed by a thick foundation, the transformation starts early every morning. Highlighting powder makes the cheek bones look bigger. Contouring makes other areas of the face look smaller. Eye liner, lip liner and eyebrow liner, some liquid and some pencil, drawn as a portrait artist. And of course, the perfect concealer can mask anything, with a blending technique using all the right tools. Mascara on the eyelashes before the falsies. The bigger the hair, the more benefits to the girdle.

129

Jacqueline loved good food and rare books. One of her treasures is the 1965 *Gay Cookbook* by Chef Lou Rand Hogan, *the complete compendium of camp cuisine and menus for men...or what have you*. Nothing made her happier than to cook for her friends and was renowned for her elaborate dinner parties and Sunday brunches. A guest would sometimes comment on a favorite book from a shelf in her living room, triggering a conversation about its acquisition, characters, writing, travel, or life memories. However, book conversations in South Beach were as rare as the books on Jacqueline's shelves.

Diego wasn't a reader, but he certainly had life memories. Jacqueline enjoyed going out to dinner with him, maybe because of the Boston connection, or maybe just good therapy for each other. They decided to head off the Beach onto the 79th Street Causeway and go to the Magnum Lounge. Jacqueline loved their puttanesca. Named after the Italian ladies of the night, she appreciated the complexity of the tomatoes and garlic simmered with anchovies, capers, olives and red pepper flakes. The piano at the bar was usually background to the conversation, but tonight they were distracted by someone new at the piano.

Her physical presence filled the room as much as her voice. This was a uniquely talented torch singer. Listening to *I Dreamed a Dream*, Diego looked over at Jacqueline as she pulled out a tissue and patted a tear. They would usually head outside to the Shack, a small lounge area which reminded them of both Key West and Cape Cod, but not tonight. She called herself The Bear and they moved to sit at stools closer to the piano to find out more about this newcomer.

She remained at the piano during her break, which gave them a chance to chat. "Have the tigers come at night my dear?" Jacqueline asked. "Not many can make the Queen of South Beach cry anymore."

"Dreams that cannot be," she said with a smile.

"Dreams made, used and wasted." Everyone sitting at the piano nodded. Contemplated.

"I have one for us. How about some Bob Fosse?" And The Bear looked at Jacqueline and sang *Maybe This Time*. By the end of the song the whole place was singing along.

As Jacqueline and Diego were leaving, she asked, "A few of us are getting together for brunch this Sunday. Would you like to join us?"

"I'd love to. That sounds nice. Here's my phone number. Oh, and by the way, I'm Judy."

Jacqueline's brunches offered plenty of food, served family style. And she made each guest feel like family. She prepared eggs Benedict with San Daniele prosciutto, fluffy ricotta pancakes, and a soppressata frittata with broccoli rabe. In her shady courtyard, her table set with white linen, fresh flowers, and beautiful silverware, each guest was presented with a Bellini cocktail. Background Italian acoustic guitar set the mood for a relaxing afternoon with some of the most uniquely interesting people in SoBe.

As Jacqueline was giving Judy a tour of the house, they stopped at her book collection, asked if she could look at two that caught her eye, and pulled the red bound books from the shelf. Jacqueline said, "Those are first editions, published by MacMillan & Company of London in 1870. I recently found out they are worth about $4,500."

She felt free to share with Jacqueline, "You know, it's because of these books I became a lyricist and confronted my dreams."

She felt free to share with Judy, "You know, it's because of these books I became true to myself and confronted my dreams, too. Sometime we will have to tell each other our stories."

"I'd like that," as she carefully put *Alice's Adventures* and *Through the Looking-Glass* back in their places of honor.

"Come try my frittata, dear. The boys here are so afraid of a little sausage fat. But wait 'til you try this Tuscan soppressata from all the leftover parts of the pig. It's exquisite." She gently brought her right hand fingers and thumb to her raised lips, kissed lightly, and tossed them into the air.

Everyone settled in the garden courtyard. Jacqueline knew Judy would be more comfortable at the head of the table. "Why don't you sit here dear, next to Diego?" She also knew he wanted to discuss a few things with Judy.

In her best Julia Child, "Bon appetit!" and everyone began to pass the eggs Benedict, the frittata, and the pancakes. Jacqueline's South Beach family was changing and growing. As she listened to the conversations at the table, she was very aware of who these people were and their influence on how the Beach was changing and growing. Again.

Jacqueline knew the history. Some of it she lived. She often joked that some of it was before her time. In the early 1900s, John Collins began building a canal and bridge to the mainland to get his avocado crop to market. In 1912, John and James Lummus saw South Beach as a resort destination and built a bathhouse. Carl Fisher finished the bridge and completed South Beach's first luxury hotel in 1913, followed by the Lincoln Road shopping district. The population grew during the Art Deco era of the 1930s and 1940s, starting a boom that lasted for decades.

When Jacqueline moved to the "sun and fun capital of the world," she often was a member of "the greatest audience in the world." From the Miami Beach Municipal Auditorium to the Fillmore Theatre in Miami Beach, she saw all the Golden Era legends. In 1964, Jackie Gleason began filming his show at the newly named Fillmore Jackie Gleason Theatre. Many a brunch story has come from Jacqueline's memories from that theater at 1700 Washington Avenue.

Warm weather, sandy beaches, sunny skies, and affordable living turned Miami Beach into a retirement community during the 1960s and 1970s. Jacqueline found Key West more to her liking until the 1980s South Beach revival. That revival began with the Mariel boatlift adding to the area's ethnic mix. The TV show *Miami Vice* brought an international interest in the pastel-colored Art Deco architecture. The LGBT community fueled the revitalization, and some of them were here at brunch, eating her frittata and drinking her Bellinis.

After the guests left, Xavier helped with the dishes. "I like Judy," he said. "Is Diego hiring her for the Anniversary Party?"

"He's trying. They were talking about it, but he couldn't say too much at the table. I wish you were with us the other night at Magnum. She is an amazing talent." She handed him the last plate, removed her rubber gloves, and smiled. "Let's go see her for our anniversary."

Five years ago, Xavier arrived in Miami for a vacation, and never left. He misses his family in Peru, but his new home is South Beach, with

Jacqueline. She has been his mentor, friend, protector, and life partner.

Xavier first met Jacqueline at the Copa. His Florida vacation included Disney World and Key West. He loved the Magic Kingdom, but by the time he got to Key West, he was ready for some serious partying. The bar went along the entire length of the dance floor, so he found an opening, got the attention of one of the bartenders, and ordered a Long Island Iced Tea. A potent equal parts gin, vodka, tequila, triple sec, sweet and sour with a splash of soda, he thought after a few of these and he would be set.

"Don't you just love watching a Long Island Iced Tea being made?" said the woman with a distinctly deep voice next to him.

Xavier looked at her, "I think he has made a few of these before." He thought she had a kind face. He had a twenty in his hand, but the kind faced woman signaled to the bartender and he went to serve someone else. "Thanks, I'm Xavier."

"You're welcome, dear. Jacqueline." She held out her hand, he went to shake it, but it moved up to his lips. "So where are you from Xavier?"

"Peru. How did you know I wasn't from here?" He sucked up about half the drink through the straw.

"Honey, no one is from here." She picked up her drink. "Would you like to join me at the

135

balcony bar? I need to sit. These new pumps are killing me!"

"Sure, lead the way." The upstairs bar had a great view of the dance floor and stage. He was already feeling the first Iced Tea as Jacqueline ordered his second.

"So tell me a little about yourself, Xavier." She reached down, took off both shoes and handed them to the bartender. "I am not going to be able to dance in them tonight!" The others at the bar laughed.

"I just graduated from Universidad De Lima. Not sure what I want to do, but there aren't many good opportunities in my country now. So here I am, getting drunk!"

"You will find no better place on the planet to get drunk than Key West. Isn't that right my friends?" Everyone agreed, and Xavier just realized that they all really were friends.

When Xavier heard that unmistakable hard kick drum and progressive base of *I Feel Love*, and Anthony Somerville's falsetto voice, he took Jacqueline's hand and they rushed down the stairs onto the dance floor. They didn't stop dancing until after Donna Summer's *Last Dance*.

House lights on, they went back upstairs to get Jacqueline's shoes. "I haven't danced that much in a long time!" she said. Outside on Duval, they chatted with some of her friends from the balcony. The warm breeze helped dry their sweaty clothes.

"Would you like to have dinner with me tomorrow night?"

"Sure, that sounds nice," Xavier smiled at her. "What time?"

"How about eight? Antonia's is a few doors down from here. One of my favorite restaurants."

"Great. I'll meet you there at eight."

She gave him a kiss on the cheek. The taxi driver opened the door, she got in, waved, and drove off. Although very attracted to him, she was relieved to be sleeping alone tonight. Well, not exactly alone.

Lucy was always curled up at her feet. The ginger tabby appeared one day at her door and there was an instant bonding. She loved being stroked and from that first day the two became inseparable.

Jack was certainly still a part of Jacqueline. Every night as she got ready for bed, there was a partial transition without the wig, makeup, and girdle. This night, he looked in the mirror and wondered how much of Jack would she share with Xavier. She hadn't thought about that in a long time.

He was waiting for her outside. She was impressed, and glad she didn't have to go into Antonia's by herself. "Good evening. Your table is ready."

"Thank you, Richard." As he pulled out her chair for her, "Craig working tonight?"

"He is. He's looking forward to seeing you."

"Wonderful. This is Xavier."

"Nice to meet you, Xavier. Enjoy your dinners."

Craig came over to welcome them, tell them about the specials and take their drink orders. The ultimate professional, he would take good care of them tonight. Candlelit tables, with a single rose at each, set the mood.

"These orange apricot roses are named after Marilyn Monroe," Jacqueline said.

"A beautiful hybrid tea rose," Xavier added. Jacqueline looked surprised.

"You know roses?"

"Yes, I love gardening and thought about becoming a Horticulturist. I worked in the greenhouses at the university."

"Ah, maybe you can help me with some of my orchids."

"Sure, they should love this climate."

"You'd think so, wouldn't you?" They both laughed.

Craig arrived with their martinis, without spilling a drop. "Enjoy these and I'll be back to take your orders." He knew Jacqueline loved a three hour dinner, and could see they were enjoying each other's company.

"So how long have you lived in Key West?"

"My home was Miami Beach, but I moved down here a few years ago. I needed to get some fun back into my life."

"Well, I certainly did have fun with you last night!"

Xavier hadn't intended on sharing that with Craig. Craig looked at Jacqueline and smiled. "May I interest you in an antipasti?"

"The antipasto with two glasses of the Veneto Prosecco Superiore?" Xavier nodded.

"Very good. I'll be back in a few minutes."

As Craig walked away, Jacqueline whispered, "Now he thinks we slept together."

Xavier leaned in and whispered back, "I wish we had."

She could feel the blood rush to her face, but the thick foundation prevented Xavier from seeing her blush, "Be patient, handsome." She put the last green olive into her mouth, just as the Prosecco and antipasto arrived.

Xavier placed some thinly sliced Genoa salami, shaved prosciutto, marinated fresh mozzarella, smoked provolone, and cantaloupe on Jacqueline's plate. He did the same for his. The fresh, crisp sparkling wine paired perfectly with the saltiness, creaminess, and sweetness.

Craig arrived, perfectly planned as usual. "How is everything?"

"Wonderful, thank you."

"May I take your pasta order?"

"Do you like clams, Xavier?"

"Love them!"

"Me too. We will have the linguini with littleneck clams."

"Wonderful choice. And a wine with your pasta?"

"What do you think, Xavier?"

"Two glasses of William Hill Chardonnay?"

"Another wonderful choice, I'll bring you a bottle," Craig smiled, "on the house. And it won't be long for your pasta."

"Thank you, Craig."

"So do you think you will move back to Miami Beach someday?"

"Oh yes, I've been thinking about it. I visit friends there often, and it's showing signs of revitalization. I have plans to go next weekend. Maybe you could join me?"

"I'd like that. Would be nice to be with someone who knows Miami."

The next course arrived and Craig poured the Chardonnay. "Would you like me to get the entre orders into the kitchen?"

"Yes, please. I'll have the yellowtail snapper."

"And for the gentleman?"

"I'll have the filet, rare."

"Very good. How are you doing with your wine?"

"I'll continue with the Chardonnay. What would you recommend with the filet?"

"The Louis Martini Cabernet Sauvignon by the glass would be nice, however we have a bottle of

Cabernet Franc which would be wonderful with the filet mignon. Oh, and also, if you are getting chocolate for dessert, it is delicious!"

"We might have to split the warm brownie then," Jacqueline said. "Bring on another bottle!"

Xavier took the last bite of brownie and emptied the wine glass. "We love good food in Peru, but I have to say, honestly, that this was one of the best meals I have ever had." He looked around the room, "And we're the last ones here. I can't believe we have been here three hours!"

Jacqueline and Xavier decided to move to Miami Beach with Lucy. She wanted to be a part of the renaissance and also thought Xavier would be happier there. They quickly became involved in the community. From auto mechanics to cake decorating, Jacqueline always loved taking the local adult continuing education classes. And it was a great way to meet people.

The School of Music at the University of Miami was offering an evening class in movement skills and dance forms from various cultures. This History of Dance course sounded interesting, as students would explore their own lives and cultures through dance, so she registered for Tuesday nights.

"Hello everyone, please call me Diego. I am a flamenco dancer from Boston. During our time together, my role will be to choreograph your histories. Let's get to know each other." And five friendships began that night.

"Can you believe it's been five years?" Jacqueline said. "I remember you standing at the bar at the Copa, ordering that Long Island Iced Tea. Such good Key West memories."

"I don't remember too much of that night! But I'll never forget the next night." Xavier reached over and gave her a kiss. "I think it would be nice to celebrate our anniversary at Magnum. I'll call Jeffrey."

They didn't leave the Beach much these days. There was no reason to. But Jacqueline wanted Xavier to hear Judy. And the puttanesca! She wore a new white dress with deco diamond earrings. He wore a light tan sport coat, white open-collar shirt with jeans. Jeffrey greeted the striking couple at the door. "Good evening my friends. Welcome and congratulations. We are glad you've chosen Magnum to celebrate."

"Thank you, Jeffrey. We've been looking forward to this night," Jacqueline said, as Xavier shook his hand.

Their candlelit table, a bottle of Perrier-Jouet and The Bear were waiting. "The Japanese anemone are beautiful," Jacqueline said smiling. Judy started to play the piano, quietly accompanying their dinner.

Plates cleared, before dessert, Judy asked for everyone's attention. "Ladies and gentlemen, we have a special couple tonight celebrating their fifth anniversary. I've been told that the night they met, they danced their asses off!" To laughter and applause, Jacqueline nodded that that was true. "And I also happen to know that their song celebrates that night and their future nights together. This is my gift to you."

Judy had prepared a vocal arrangement that Whitney herself would have loved. As she began singing *I Wanna Dance With Somebody Who Loves Me*, Xavier stood, took Jacqueline's hand and they danced playfully, inviting others to join them. And then Judy began to sing a capella *I Will Always Love You*. As they swayed to the most romantic song ever, holding each other tight, Jacqueline mouthed a thank you to Judy.

Back at their table, Jacqueline patted dry the line of tears. How does Judy do this to her? But before she had a chance to think about it too much, Jeffrey arrived with the Crêpes Suzette dessert cart as the lights dimmed. He caramelized the butter and sugar, added orange juice and folded the crepes into the boiling sweetness. Grand Marnier is carefully poured over the crêpes and flambéed. He plates each serving with a scoop of homemade vanilla ice cream.

The perfect romantic dinner complete, they went over to sit with Judy at the piano as she was completing her Broadway set. "Thank you so much for singing our song. We will never forget this night."

"Xavier wanted this to be a very special night. I think he succeeded." Judy smiled at him.

"Are you still going to the Warsaw rehearsal?" Jacqueline asked. "Diego expects this to be memorable!"

"I'll go to the rehearsal, but I haven't committed to the event yet. I'm a little nervous about it."

"Don't be, hon. Diego thinks the world of you. Plus, you never know who will be there. David Padilla has put the place on the dance music map."

"Yes, I'm looking forward to meeting him."

"So I'll pick you up at 2:30, OK dear?"

Jeffrey had their car waiting. They waved goodbye and drove back to the Beach with the top down. From NE 79th Street onto the JFK Causeway, where the moon had risen over Pelican Harbor, the warm ocean breeze was amplified by Mustang speed and a champagne buzz.

When they arrived back at the apartment, wind-blown and disheveled, they left a trail of ripped-off clothes and jewelry toward the bed. A sport jacket, shirt, heels, shoes, socks, a dress, pantyhose, a belt, jeans, bra, necklace, girdle, some underwear, and a wig. The transition was just as intense as the first time, five years ago.

144

Jack woke Xavier with a cup of coffee and a kiss. He had already picked up, folded or hung the remnants of their celebration, and started some laundry. "Buenos dias, guapo!"

"Buenos dias, guapa! Gracias por el café," taking a sip, "This afternoon should be interesting."

"I've seen a lot on the Beach over the years, but Diego has something planned that will set the bar for all future events here."

"Working at Warsaw gets more interesting by the night, that's for sure!"

"Just remain vigilant, Xavi. Especially as they challenge the police. You know, disappear into the crowd."

"Oh I know, don't worry about me." But she did. The Warsaw was receiving numerous warnings, citations and fines from the city as the shows got more decadent, which might attract the attention of INS agents.

"I've heard Peru is lovely this time of year."

"Very funny." Xavier didn't want to think about the possibility.

It took Jacqueline a little longer than usual to get ready, but she looked in the full length mirror and liked what she saw. "Xavi, I'm off to pick up Judy. See you tonight!"

"OK, don't forget to move the passenger seat all the way back and adjust the seatbelt."

She fit, but they didn't bother with the seatbelt. Rationalized because it wasn't that long a drive.

145

"Do you have any idea what Diego has planned for this party?" Judy asked.

"He has run a few things by me, but by now I'm sure he has the night sequenced and visualized in that imaginative, crazy mind of his." Diego was waiting to greet them.

"Welcome to Warsaw!" he said to Judy. "Come meet your fellow Seduction players. Some you know from brunch."

Jacqueline had never seen the inside of this notorious building without its club crowds. The air conditioned, dark space gave her a chill. She felt better seeing familiar faces and went over to chat with the dancers while watching Judy and Nelson follow Diego to the stage. From behind the curtain, she heard Judy's "No, no, no, no!" and went to investigate.

"Where did you ever get that?" impressed, Jaqueline said, with the emphasis on the "that". The "that" was a ten-foot, gold-colored, fiberglass penis.

"It's on loan from Naomi Wilzig's collection," Diego said, proudly. "She has been on a 15-year quest collecting erotic art from around the world. This will make its debut at the Anniversary Party."

Jacqueline had a new wig, dress, and pumps that would be making their debut for the Anniversary. The quaffed bleach-blond changed it up a bit with new bangs and a flip. She found a stunning leopard print retro dress with spaghetti straps and an elegant black high heel at Merle's Closet. She put on her vintage leopard earrings and Xavier helped her with the matching pendant necklace. They put Lucy in her soft-sided pet tote and headed out to work.

Everyone was early. The house lights were on. The front doors were still locked and a line had begun to form. The girls were in their dressing room primping with Judy. The boys were doing pushups with Diego. Nelson was excited. The bartenders and barbacks were setting up. David was in his booth with the lighting and sound technician. Jacqueline was in her booth with Lucy. The house lights dimmed and Jaime announced "Happy Anniversary, everyone!" and opened the front doors.

The line had absorbed into the Ballroom, now at capacity, and Jacqueline was finally able to take a break. Diego came to relieve her, knowing that Elaine Lancaster would be taking the stage any minute. It took her a while to get to the bar. "The usual, Miss Jacqueline?"

"Yes please, Shawn," as she stood in pain from her new shoes. Still, it was the perfect viewing spot for the show. She took a sip of her Mai Tai just as drag Cher was escorted on stage. She thought, that girl has balls showing off her ass like that!

Before heading back to her booth, Jacqueline wanted to see an old friend, on vacation from New York, up in the VIP lounge. A very deserving VIP from the Nederlander Organization and Broadway Cares/Equity Fights AIDS.

With outstretched arms, the two hugged and kissed. "Junior!" Jacqueline said, "It's so good to see you."

"My dear, dear girl, how have you been?" he said. "Come sit and have a drink with us."

"I'd love to. I can't stay too long, but I'd love to," and signaled to the waiter. "Jeff up here makes a pretty mean Mai Tai."

"And how's that handsome Xavier?"

"He's great. Working downstairs. I'm sure you'll see him before the end of the night." It was time to ask Junior, while they were talking about the end of the night. "Wait until you hear the closing performance, Junior. If you have time, please come to Judy's dressing room and I will introduce you."

"For you dear, anything." They talked a while longer before she had to finish up in her booth.

Xavier took his break with Jacqueline as the Party was coming to an end. They held hands as the floodlight hits Judy, singing Gloria Gaynor's *I Will Survive*, that message of defiance, Broadway bound.

JUDY

The Pied Piper is known for its "After Tea" in Provincetown. The summer revelers move up Commercial Street from the Boatslip to the Pied to continue drinking and dancing. Before that last dance up the street, the waterfront women's bar is quiet. Judy loved the late afternoon gig there. Her piano was positioned looking out at the expansive outdoor deck, with a view of MacMillan Pier and Cape Cod Bay.

Known as The Bear, she sang torch songs that touched her audience in a special way. Looking like Mama Cass and sounding like Linda Ronstadt, she had a committed summer following in P-town.

Judy was renting a one room cottage with a sleep loft on Commercial Street. The climb up the ladder at night and down in the morning was a worthwhile challenge. From her small deck she could see Long Point Light. With art galleries as her neighbors, this was the quieter end of town.

The Mews Restaurant was an easy walk. The Bear performed on Sunday nights in the upstairs lounge and always brought some food home for a late second dinner. The lobster vindaloo was her favorite. A Cape Cod twist on the traditional Indian dish had lobster chunks in a spicy tangy curry sauce served with tomato chutney, naan, basmati rice, broccoli, heirloom carrots and fennel. She poured

150

herself a glass of Riesling to balance the spice. The Riesling would pair nicely with dessert. Triple espresso gelato sandwiched between two large semi-sweet dark & white Belgian chocolate chip cookies, drizzled with dark chocolate ganache. She finished the bottle and wouldn't bother climbing the ladder tonight.

Sunrise was her favorite time of day. Coffee sipped with the oldsquaw and her thoughts. As the peeking sun began to reflect on the calmness, the quiet interrupted only by the random kazoo-like calls, her inner voice decided this summer would be all about creativeness and acceptance. Then the same voice told her she was full of shit. Some things are not acceptable.

As long as Judy could remember, she had always wanted to write her own songs. And as long as Judy could remember, she had always hated her own body. Creativeness and acceptance is Provincetown, so why not be content with interpretation and good food? Maybe this summer would be all about contentedness. And yet, there were those recurring dreams...Sitting on the piano bench, her legs dangled under the keys. Unable to reach the pedals, the offer was enticing to Judy's instructor, touching thigh to thigh. It would be their secret.

In the heart of the East End Gallery District, across the street from the Provincetown Art Museum, was Angel Foods. Before Commercial Street got too crazy, she would take an early walk to her favorite market to pick up a few things. "Good morning, good morning everyone," almost singing her greeting. "What did you make for soups, Anita?"

"Oh, we have your favorite Portuguese kale, dear," paused and waited for the smile. "A delicious gazpacho and our famous clam chowder."

"Feels like it's gonna be a warm one. I'll have a large gazpacho and four crab cakes, thanks. I'll walk around a bit."

"See you at the register. By the way, we have those Spanish fig cakes you like."

"Oh my god, they are so delicious!" she grabbed a basket and started to browse. Two bottles of Rioja Gran Reserva, some Churro Zamorano cheese, some tart cherry and cacao nib crostini, two warm cranberry and blueberry muffins, and of course, a Spanish fig cake, and she was done. Anita was waiting at the register. "All the makings of a nice lunch here. Think you can join me on the deck?"

"You know, I think I will. Mind if it's after the rush?"

"Of course not. Get you off your feet for a bit."

"Thanks my friend. I'll see you at around 1:30."

Commercial Street was coming to life. Dogs being walked, delivery trucks trying to park, coffees after a fun night, and everyone saying their good mornings. The Pied and Mews gigs were giving her a much needed recognition. Judy couldn't think of a better place to be on the planet.

The uneven bricked sidewalk was getting more difficult to maneuver. Negotiating the two-way pedestrian traffic was almost impossible on a busy summer day, so she would alternate between street and sidewalk and was always relieved to arrive at her destination. She put her food away and made another pot of coffee. It was a nice morning to do some reading.

A few days ago, after a few delicious margaritas, Judy had stopped in for her weekly browsing at the Provincetown Public Library. Built in 1873, with its two sloped mansard roof, the Library is a nationally registered historic place. Interestingly, its top floor housed a meeting place for a temperance society, the Chequocket Lodge No. 76, Independent Order of Good Templars. Influenced by the tequila, she checked out Lewis Carroll's *Alice's Adventures in Wonderland* and *Through the Looking Glass*. She was looking forward to having some fun reading these books, and wondered if there was an organization called the Independent Order of Bad Templars.

She put her cup of coffee and muffins onto the side table and settled into one of the Adirondack chairs. Anita made a damn good muffin, she thought, looking forward to their lunch together. When she opened her book, there was a slight musty smell mixing with the sea air. She wondered who had read this book before her. She looked at the illustration of the White Rabbit and loved that Alice has the curiosity to follow it down the hole. Maybe to be able to "shut up like a telescope!" If she only knew how to begin. "For, you see, so many out-of-the-way things had happened lately, that Alice had begun to think that very few things indeed were really impossible." She stopped. Looked out at the bay. Reread the sentences. Stopped again. And just thought a while.

"Hello dear, rise and shine!" Anita startled her, wiping the drool from her chin.

"Oh my god, what time is it? I can't believe I fell asleep," looking at her watch, she got up to give her friend a hug. "Make yourself comfortable. Would you like some wine or an iced tea?"

Fitting just perfectly into the chair, "Thank you so much. I'm exhausted! We sold about fifty sandwiches. You know I love the tips, but I can't wait 'til September. I could use a glass of wine."

"Wonderful. I'll be right back." She poured two glasses and arranged some crostini and cheese on a plate and returned outside. "I hope you have some time to relax before the dinner rush."

"I can stay for an hour or so. What time do you start at the Pied?"

"I like to get there a little before 3:00. Had a small group arrive by sailboat yesterday. I hope they come back today."

"I love this little beach cottage. Is this part of Dave and Steve's Aerie House up on Bradford Street?"

"It is. They call it the Beach Club. I like that I can do my vocal warm-ups without bothering too many people. The only problem is that damn ladder to the loft after a few drinks." They both laughed, but Judy did wonder if the futon was going to be the only option as the summer progressed. It wasn't the few drinks that was the problem. "I hope you're hungry."

Judy headed into the kitchen to prepare lunch. She brought out two bowls of gazpacho and plates of crab cakes and potato salad. "This look familiar?" as she poured more Rioja.

"I can't think of a better lunch and a better person to have it with." They clinked their glasses together, "To a great summer!"

Washing down the last pieces of crab cake by emptying their wine glasses, Anita sighs. "I wish I could stay longer but it's time for us to serve the Provincetown throngs." She cleared the table and asked, "I'm going to have Sasha take my shift tomorrow night. Would you like to grab some dinner and maybe see a show?"

"That sounds so nice. Would be wonderful to see someone else perform. We could walk into town from here. What time's good for you?"

"I can be ready at sixish. Thanks so much again for lunch," as the two hugged each other tight then kissed, crossing the friendship line.

It was time to get ready for the Pied. Time for her ritual voice exercises. To decrease vocal cord puffiness, she would blow into a small stirring straw while phonating up and down her range. Without the straw she would do lip trills. She would ascend into her upper register using the nay sound. Neighbors would hear the strangest sounds coming from her cottage. Creaky doors, hooty gees, coo coos, googs and mums, and finally ooh-oh-uh-ahs while putting on her makeup and getting dressed.

She strolled down Commercial Street, peeking in store and gallery windows and stopped at the Crown & Anchor's signboard. The Crown would be a great place to take in a show with Anita. Built in the mid-19th century as the Central House, it was now the town's "largest entertainment complex". With its grand columned portico and tower, the Reed father and son years saw the Central enlarged as a public hall for shows, a bowling alley, and more importantly, a saloon.

Jimmy James Brings Marilyn Monroe to Provincetown was the headline. Perfect. No lip syncing. Judy had met Jimmy James a few times around town and promised she would see his show. His Eartha Kitt, Billie Holiday, Patsy Cline, Bette Davis, Judy Garland, Barbra Streisand, Cher, and of course Marilyn were becoming nationally renowned. She knew the early show and dinner would be a memorable evening.

Michael and Andy entered the Pied at the end of the long wood-planked walkway. Judy had already begun her set. They both had looked forward to seeing The Bear again, so it seemed appropriate that she was singing Carly Simon's *Anticipation*. Sometimes they wondered about still being together tomorrow, or how right tonight might be. Still, it was obvious to everyone in the room that Judy loved singing this song. She gave Michael a big smile and transitioned into *Coming Around Again*. Impressed, Michael smiled back.

The Bear finished up her last set and DJ Maryalice started spinning. The Boatslip line was forming at the door, checking IDs and collecting the cover. "Let's dance a while," Michael told Andy. They finished their drinks and joined the growing "After-Tea" crowd. The Hat Sisters made their entrance, looking as fabulous as ever!

John and Tim brought joy and laughter to a community raw with grief and helplessness. In the midst of the AIDS crisis, they would often appear at three fundraisers a day, wearing identical themed spectacular hats. Sometimes three to four feet high, stitched, glue-gunned, sewed or Velcroed

157

with Barbie Dolls, feathers, balloons, starships, swans, teddy bears, or other countless creations with matching dresses and heels, it was always a welcome sight to see the hats bouncing to the rhythm over the dance floor crowd.

In her perfectly fitting, white sequined gown, Marilyn stretched her arms towards the audience and blows Judy and Anita a kiss with her heart-shaped voluptuous crimson lips. She stands at the microphone as the guitarist begins with a quiet introduction of a very familiar arpeggiated, finger-picked chord progression which, at first, dissociates the audience. She appears to begin to sing, but in a typical Marilyn tease, decides to wait a few bars. And then, in her breathy, slightly off-key voice, she sings about that lady buying a stairway to heaven. The experience makes the audience wonder. Judy and Anita look at each other. Wonderstruck.

Although Judy would have to climb the stairs, a late romantic dinner at Café Edwige would give them an opportunity to enjoy a nice conversation. Edwige was one of their favorite restaurants in town. They ordered fried Wellfleet oysters, blackened tuna tataki with beech mushrooms, butter-poached lobster with squid ink risotto, coquille St. Jacques with gruyere and cognac, and a bottle of white Burgundy Montrachet.

Amused to see Absinthe on the dessert menu, they thought it might be fun to join Toulouse-Lautrec, Vincent van Gogh, and Oscar Wilde in their explorations of the complex, floral flavors. After all, Wilde had described the hallucinogenic sensation of tulips brush against his legs after leaving a bar at closing. They ordered two Jade Nouvelle Orleans and summoned the Green Fairy.

The next morning, Anita helped Judy down the ladder. "Three more steps, hon." Anita thought it shouldn't be so difficult getting in and out of bed.

"Want some coffee out on the deck?"

"That sounds nice. I'll have to head home, take a shower, and go to the store. But some coffee to start the day, thanks."

With the sound of Judy grinding the beans, she yelled out to the deck, "What an amazing night. Jimmy James was brilliant! We should go see him again."

"Absolutely. I heard he changes it up. Would love to hear his Patsy Cline."

As they enjoyed their morning coffee, and each other's company, Anita asked "When's your next day off?"

"I was just going to ask you the same thing," smiling back. "I might take on another gig at the piano bar at the Gifford House on Wednesday nights."

"Oh, that would be perfect for you. Want to come over to my house for dinner Thursday?"

"I'd love to. I'll bring the wine."

Anita got up and gave Judy a kiss. "Don't get up. Enjoy your coffee, hon. Maybe I'll come in and see you at the Pied if the store is slow."

And so the summer of contentedness continued. During one of her Commercial Street walks, Judy purchased a writing journal from the Provincetown Bookshop. She was feeling poetic these days and some self-therapy couldn't hurt. Maybe there was a song or two to share with The Bear's fans. She had been thinking about Grace Slick and listening intently to her voice lately. She decided to add *White Rabbit* to her Pied gig next week. If Marilyn could sing *Stairway to Heaven*, she could sing *White Rabbit*. Maybe she could follow with *Somebody to Love*. As she sat looking out onto the bay, she opened her new journal and started to think about how she had found somebody to love. Even though she knew she was going to fall, would she still chase the rabbit?

Although she had finished reading them, she would stop by the library on her way to the Pied and renew the Carroll books. That damn hookah-smoking caterpillar wasn't done with her. First page, center of the top line she wrote the three words...Who are YOU? She got up and went inside to the kitchen. If she was going to have a conversation with a caterpillar, she would need more coffee and an Angel's chocolate croissant or two.

She picked up the *Adventures*, opened to page 22 and read "I-I hardly know, sir, just at present- at least I know who I WAS when I got up this morning, but I think I must have been changed several times since then."

"What do you mean by that?" said the Caterpillar sternly. "Explain yourself!"

"I can't explain MYSELF, I'm afraid, sir" said Alice, "because I'm not myself, you see."

"I don't see," said the Caterpillar.

"I'm afraid I can't put it more clearly," Alice replied very politely, "for I can't understand it myself to begin with; and being so many different sizes in a day is very confusing."

She closed the book and wanted to write something. Was she afraid? She remembered a favorite professor at Berklee College of Music that encouraged free association writing as a technique to clear your head or focus your thoughts. Sometimes mundane, sometimes profound. Those three cathartic words. Who are YOU?

I am a woman. A musician. A piano player. The Bear. Lesbian. Someone who loves to perform. Appreciates good food and wine. A reader. A writer? Where will I be in one year, five years? What is happening with Anita? Big, beautiful. Abused. Sexually. Not sure I want to do this. Don't stop. Why me? Back to me. Who am I? I see the way people look at me. Sometimes recognition and gratitude. Sometimes disgust. Do I have control over that? Sometimes. Should I write poetry or lyrics? Is there a difference? I see the way people respond when I am performing other musician's songs? Can I get the same response to my own? Worth the risk. Perfect spot to write. Water calms me. What will be my favorite memory of this summer? Who are my fans? Am I a torch singer? Diva? Do I want to write happy or sad or both? Why are there so many questions?

Judy put her pen down and takes a sip of coffee. So now what? She turns the page to find some answers. In her mind she hears F sharp, the minor third, and the fifth from *White Rabbit*. Picks up the pen and writes...

Not sure I want to do this.

Don't stop. Why me? Back to me.

Who am I?

I see the way people look at me.

Do I have control over that?

Sometimes.

She thinks this was a good start and decides to commit to mornings as her writing time. Every morning, no excuses. But how much of herself was she willing and able to share as a song writer? She was still afraid, but she felt safe with her Provincetown fans, so down the hole she would go.

Anita lives in a West End Floater with a view from Long Point to Wood End. From East to West was a long walk for Judy, so Anita sent a horse-drawn carriage to pick her up. Judy waved to the Commercial Street summer crowds as they called out "The Bear!", and she realized that it appeared to be promotional rather than an act of affection. Either way, she was just fine with it.

The driver helped Judy from the carriage. Anita came out to greet her. "Thanks Kevin. How about noon tomorrow?" She put some money in his hand. "Come on in, hon." She opened the gate to the white picket fence, and they walked the brick path to the front door. The blue and white ceramic tile with a house on a boat was to the right. As they entered, Judy felt the warmness of the original wide pine floors and the whitewashed beamed ceiling. "Let's go to the back deck. There's a nice sea breeze out there." On the way they stopped in the kitchen. "This is a delicious Russian River Chardonnay. Should I pour us some?"

"Of course. Is there anything I can do to help?" looking around the kitchen. "You have been very busy I see."

"An oyster stew, and a few more Cape Cod classics that are fun to prepare. I sometimes wonder what the families ate in this house after they floated it over from Long Point."

"Are those Parker House rolls?"

"They are. Wait 'til you see what I have planned for them," smiling. "And Boston Cream pie. My favorite dessert."

"Oh yes! Mine too."

Anita had created a very comfortable seating area on the deck. As they sipped their wine, Judy told her about the free association writing experience. "I'm going to spend the rest of the summer composing and try a few new songs at the Pied. Time to start using what I learned at Berklee."

"Might be time to get yourself an agent," Anita said, as she got up to get two bowls of stew from the kitchen. "I used freshly shucked Wellfleets and of course, some bacon," sharing an Angel secret.

Judy scooped up an oyster and put the sweet, smoky, firm meat into her mouth. Surrounded by the milky wine and butter, the briny Wellfleet harbor was released as she chewed and swallowed. "Oh my god!" and went for oyster number two.

As promised, Anita presented her plan for the Parker House rolls. Using her homemade dill tartar sauce, she prepared cod sandwiches with bacon, lettuce and tomatoes from her garden. "This is my nana's recipe for cod cheeks and tongues. I thought it would make a nice sandwich."

"I never actually thought of fish as having tongues," Judy laughed as she took a bite. "Oh yes, this is delicious!"

The master bedroom was up the spiral staircase, so they had to sleep in the guest suite downstairs. Anita woke up first and brought them some coffee in bed. She was a little disappointed they weren't upstairs to see the sunrise over the bay. "I have to get to the store, hon. Relax here, maybe take a soak in the tub and do some writing. There are some blueberry muffins in the kitchen. Kevin will be by to pick you up at noon, OK?"

"That sounds great. It will be wonderful to take a bath for a change."

"I'll call you later. Love you."

"Love you, too." They kissed and Anita was off to open the store.

She turned on the water to the large clawfoot tub. Anita had a selection of Provincetown Soap Works products. The Coastal Breeze Dead Sea Bath Salts caught her eye. She used the cockleshell to pour two scoops into the warm water and wondered about her displacement. As she lowered herself into the mineral and botanical bath, she closed her eyes and a feeling of complete surrender overcame her almost constant conscious struggle. Was pleasure conflicting with the meditative state? She thought...probably. What the fuck. Just go with it.

September was the nicest month in Provincetown, unless you were trying to earn a living. Judy had Saturday and Sunday afternoons at the Pied, and Sunday night at the Mews. She would rent the cottage for October and then move on. "Where are you going for the winter?" was the common inquiry. Back to school, Boston, New York or Key West were the common responses. But Judy had started to hear more about Miami Beach. She thought she would rent again in Key West, and during the winter visit South Beach. She wondered how this conversation would go with Anita.

Transition might as well be celebrated with a classic New England lobster boil, and they could think of no better place than the Lobster Pot. At a table overlooking the harbor, they would talk about their future over a P-town paella covered with a couple of selects. And a bottle of wine, of course. Any frustration could be taken out on the lobster. As Anita ripped the claws from the body, she asks, "So is there any way I can talk you out of going to Key West?"

"Any way I can talk you into moving to Key West?" They laughed. "You know you can come down anytime, escape the snow and cold."

"I just might do that. Sasha can handle the store."

"And I'll be back in May. Provincetown is starting to feel like home to me."

"I hope I had a little to do with that."

"A little?" She took Anita's hand. "This is the happiest I've been in a long time, and it's because of you."

Anita looked down at their conjoined hands coated in the lemony congealed hemolymph, "I think this relationship can survive a short physical separation."

Judy rented a two-bedroom cottage on Olivia Street, right in the center of Old Town Key West. A shotgun style conch, she would be just a block from Duval, near the Hemingway Home. Early settlers of the Florida Keys built their homes of a mortar made from sand, water, and lime. The lime came from burning conch shells. Often the shell itself was used in constructing the houses. Later, the architectural style took on the name of conch house. Some say the name shotgun came because a bullet fired through the front door would go right out the backdoor without hitting a wall. However, some think that the name comes from shogon. In West Africa, shogon means "God's House." Not sure about that, at only about twelve feet wide, it would be another rabbit-hole for Judy.

In 1892, Teodoro Perez built his main house at 1125 Duval Street. His cigar factory faced Simonton and cottages for the workers on Catherine. He was best known for his support for the revolutionists in Cuba, supplying them with money and arms to support Jose Marti. In May of that year, Marti gave speeches from the second floor balcony

167

overlooking Duval. Key West locals now hang out at La Terraza de Marti or La Te Da.

The Bear performed every Friday night at the former Perez Residence, in what is now the Hotel Lobby and Piano Bar of La Te Da. Permanently parked out front was an iconic 1959 pink Cadillac convertible. So she felt obligated to tell its story through Natalie Cole's voice, and most listening appreciated the oozing of the *Pink Cadillac* on a Friday night.

Her Mews routine well established, La Te Da also had dinner-to-go ready at the end of each gig. Once home, she decided to eat outside on the porch and opened a Loire Valley Cabernet Franc. The Domaine de la Chevalerie Bourgueil would be perfect with the blue cheese and herb-encrusted filet mignon. She emptied the bottle into the full, round glass and took the last few bites of mashed potato and asparagus. As the bowl allowed the wine to come in contact with the tropical Key West salty air, Judy wondered how the same glass of wine would taste in the chilly Provincetown salty air.

Day-to-day tasks in her P-town cottage, except for that damn ladder, were easier in the open, square room. The Key West rectangular shotgun often involved adding to her bruised thighs as she maneuvered from living room to kitchen to bedroom. She'd relax and enjoy the nice warm night before bringing the dishes inside. And think about Anita.

Anita had never been to Key West. Winter was slow at Angel Foods, a perfect time for a vacation. When the taxi stopped at Olivia Street she couldn't believe how adorably tiny the house was. And as she squeezed Judy tight at the top of the stairs, she couldn't believe how adorably large her woman was.

"Welcome to the Conch Republic!" Judy laughed. "Come on in. I'll give you the grand tour of how the cigar makers used to live."

Anita left her two suitcases out on the porch because she wasn't sure if there would be enough room. She followed Judy into the living room. "Oh, this is so nice. Such a welcome escape from the cold Cape air. I might stay 'til spring!"

"Turn your two weeks into two months! Call Sasha now," smiling, she picked up the phone.

"Show me the place first," she said, nervous about the two weeks.

"Well, you can see why they call these houses shotguns. Nothing stopping a bullet from going through the living room to the kitchen, bathroom and bedroom." Anita looked out to the back porch. "Let's have some iced tea out back. It's my favorite part of the house."

"That sounds perfect. I'll get my bags."

The Hemmingway House down the street attracted sidewalk traffic, so the magenta bougainvillea vine provided a private oasis at the back patio. Judy brought out two large Mexican blue rim glasses filled with ice and she poured the lemon infused sun tea. "Thank you, hon." The cushioned, white wicker love seat felt so comfortable to Anita after being cramped in an airplane seat for hours.

"I was thinking we could go for a trolley ride after you take a nap. It's kinda touristy but a quick way to see the island and get your bearings. Then Antonia's for dinner if you want."

"I'd love a nap, but only if you join me," Anita said, with that smile that drove Judy crazy.

They walked to the Bahama Village Market, where the green and orange Old Town Trolley picked them up. The route brought them out past Smathers Beach, Southernmost Point, and back down Duval to Mallory Square and Sloppy Joe's Bar.

"Let's get off here. I want you to meet a few friends and we can have a Pirate Punch or two before dinner. You will love this place! It used to be an icehouse and the morgue. Wait 'til you see the hanging tree!" Judy looked over at Anita for the expected reaction.

Anita tries to take it all in. *The Oldest Bar in Florida*, The First and Original Sloppy Joe's 1933-1937, The Hemingway Years Spent Here, Elect

Capt. Tony Tarracino Mayor, the dollar bills, license plates, and the bras. The bras.

Captain Tony met Judy with a hug and kiss. She turns to Anita, "This man ate the last mango in Paris. Anita, meet the Mayor of Key West, Captain Tony. Captain, this is Anita." The old salty dog planted one on Anita, too.

He tells Becky, "Get these ladies a couple of Pirate Punches on the house! Have a seat here at the tree and she'll bring your drinks right over."

Becky gets to work quickly mixing 2 oz gin, 2 oz dark rum, 2 tsp sugar, 2 oz fresh lemon juice, 4 oz fresh lime juice, 8 oz pineapple juice, 4 oz OJ, a splash of 7up, and a dash of bitters. She then garnishes the Capt. Tony's cups with orange slices and cherries, shakes well and pours the famous punch over ice.

"Thanks Tony. Hey, when you coming to see me at La Te Da?"

"You get your bras up on the wall here, and I'll come see ya." Two of the three laughed. Becky delivered the Punches.

"Anita, this is Becky, the best bartender in town."

"Nice to meet you," as they suck the fruity rum into their mouths. "Oh my god, this is delicious!"

"Told you! Wait 'til you see her creations up at the Copa's balcony. We'll head there tomorrow night. You know, maybe we should leave a bit of ourselves here though."

"You'd be in good company. Hemingway, Capote, Williams, Silverstein, and Buffett have all drank here." Becky was trying to encourage the donations. "I hope you have your business cards on you." She looked around for the step ladder.

"Ok, let's do this!" Anita looked at Judy and said to Becky, raising her empty glass, "Two more please."

With a stealth precision, the two brassieres appeared on the table, much to the approval of the Captain. Becky stapled the business cards to the cups, climbed the ladder, and looped them around the beam.

"Hopefully, the Lady in Blue approves." Becky looks around the bar and carefully descends and goes to pour two more Pirate Punches.

"The Lady in Blue?" Anita looked around, too.

Becky delivers the punches and asks, "You sure you want to hear about her?" They nod their heads and suck up a few ounces. "Well, many years before the Captain was even born, the local hanging tree was conveniently located right next to the morgue. One night, the woman in the blue dress killed her husband and two boys. She chopped them up and dragged their body parts into the back yard for the animals to dispose of."

"Damn!" Anita said.

Becky continued, "A neighbor saw what she did and called the police. When the police arrived, the woman was lying on her bed in a blue nightgown

172

covered in blood. They immediately brought her to the hanging tree and hanged her. A few years later, a big storm washed away the morgue. Captain Tony's was then built around the hanging tree on top of the old morgue. During excavation, several bodies were found, and with no money to relocate them, the concrete was poured on top and bottles of holy water inserted into the concrete. The ghost is supposedly of the woman in the blue dress."

"Damn!" Anita said, again.

"Yeah, you two are probably sitting on her right now."

Antonia's on Duval would be the perfect ending to Anita's first day. In the front window, pasta is made every morning and hung to dry. Judy knew Anita would appreciate this elegant and beloved little Italian restaurant.

"Good evening ladies. My name is Craig and I'll be your server tonight. May I get you something to drink?"

Judy looked at Anita and asked, "Martinis?"

"Oh yes!"

"Two Hendricks with an olive," smiling.

"Sounds wonderful, I'll be right back with them."

They started with an antipasto and plump and tender helix escargots, paired with a Piemonte Chardonnay, Costeblanche Coppo.

"I can't wait to see you perform at La Te Da on Friday. I wonder if Captain Tony will show."

173

"Oh, I hope so, but Friday might be difficult for him to leave the Saloon." The waiter poured their second glasses.

"Ladies, would you like to order your main courses now? All of our pasta is made fresh daily," Craig reminded them.

"We would like to first share the linguine with Key West pink shrimp while we finish our Chardonnay. And then the local grouper with a bottle of Pinot Grigio. What would you recommend?"

"I like the Santa Margherita from Alto Adige. You'll love it with the key lime beurre blanc."

"Nice, thanks Craig."

The next day, after breakfast at Blue Heaven, Anita went out exploring on her own, knowing it would be too much walking for Judy. She wanted to make some Key West business connections for Angel Foods. She met with Key West Key Lime Pie Co, The Cookie Lady, and Key West Aloe. Everyone agreed that the Provincetown customers would love their products.

Back at the shotgun, Anita and Judy relaxed at the shaded patio with some chicory coffee and, of course, some key lime pie. "I met The Cookie Lady today!"

"Ah yes, Marilyn. She has been trying to talk me into performing at Sunset. We can go to Mallory Dock tonight if you want."

174

"I'd love that. Bagpipes playing as the sun sets. Doesn't get more romantic than that." She gives Judy a kiss on her way to get more coffee for them. "You thinking of performing at sunset?"

"No, I don't think it's for me. Too crowded. And I like my audience sitting, not walking by."

"Yeah, I get that."

"I was thinking of renting a convertible and us driving to Miami Beach for a few days to check out the scene there."

"That sounds great. Maybe this weekend after your La Te Da gig."

They looked at each other and in unison, "Road trip!"

They traveled through Boca Chica, Sugarloaf, Summerland, Ramrod, Big Pine, on the Seven Mile Bridge, Vaca, Marathon, Long, Fiesta, Matecumbe, Islamorada, Windley, and Key Largo, to Route 1 North, arriving in Miami Beach almost four hours later. The windblown women pulled up to the Cavalier Hotel on Ocean Drive, in awe of the Art Deco masterpiece that would be their home for the next few days. Designed by architect Roy France in 1936, they were welcomed by a lobby of beautiful furniture, nautical themed decorations and eclectic art pieces.

Escorted up to their room with a king size bed and an ocean view, "Oh I think this will do nicely."

Anita looked at the bellhop and Judy, smiling and tipping generously. "Any recommendations for what we should do first to get the feel for this place?" she asked him.

"Happy hours at either the News or the Front Porch are great to meet some locals and people watch. Tell them Gino sent you and they will take good care of you."

He was right. A sidewalk table was waiting at the News Café and it was 2-4-1! The waiter recommended one of their real hand-carved coconut drinks...a Beach Baby. Cruzan Pineapple and Coconut Rum, orange Rum, lemonade, and orange juice. They ordered some ceviche, coconut shrimp, and conch fritters, sat back and watched the beautiful people walk by.

Judy browsed through *Around Town* magazine and saw an ad for the Magnum Lounge off the 79th Street Causeway. The "sultry piano bar in Miami's trendy Upper East Side" sounded interesting. She showed the page to Anita, "We might have to check this place out."

Anita read, "An eclectic group of customers who tend to sing along and have a fabulous time," looking up at Judy. "Oh yeah, that sounds like your fans!"

"Let's ask Gino if he knows anything about the food, maybe go to dinner tomorrow night?"

Gino loved their puttanesca, so he made a reservation for them. It was a nice drive off the

Beach, in the Design District. They were greeted at the door by Jeffrey. "Hello ladies. Welcome to Magnum," looking at Judy, "I am a huge fan of yours. I saw you perform in Provincetown this summer. Would you like to sit near the piano?" hopefully anticipating a yes.

"Just in case?" Judy asked, thinking she liked him and his place. "Sure, we always love sitting near a piano!"

Jeffrey recommended the Falanghina Greco from Campania. They ordered the crab quesadilla and two conch chowders and the avocado with crabmeat. The puttanesca was as good as Gino said it was. Jeffrey joined them for dessert, on the house. "I would be honored if you would sing a few songs tonight," he said.

The customers had a fabulous time with The Bear's Ronstadt set. Jeffrey made Judy a very generous offer to pay for her flights from Key West until she found a place on the Beach. This was indeed generous because she required two seats.

After breakfast at the hotel, they met with a realtor to look at a few apartments and returned to the News for lunch. "I liked that place with the fountain courtyard. First floor, big, newly renovated, and less than I'm paying now."

"I think you have to do it, hon. Winter in Key West. It doesn't suck to be you!"

177

With the roof down again, they drove back onto the Seven Mile Bridge and arrived back in Key West just in time for Tea.

Anita had less than a week before she had to go back up north and that time would fly by. Judy would start at Magnum when she left. Friday night they went to La Te Da. One last sunset on Saturday night.

The taxi arrived at the shotgun to take Anita to the airport. "Well hon, springtime will be here real fast. I love you so much."

"I love you, too. I hope you don't have too many snowstorms until then." They kissed and squeezed each other tight.

Judy took a taxi from the airport to Magnum. Jeffrey had an available apartment upstairs for her to stay anytime she wanted.

The piano was built into the bar, giving a closeness that The Bear wasn't used to at her other gigs. She had worked on a new set of Broadway tunes and decided to start with Sondheim's *Losing My Mind* and *Send in the Clowns*. Good choices. The room was hers now.

Time for her Wonderland connection. In a voice soft as thunder, *I Dreamed a Dream* brought tears to some. She nodded an understanding to one particular woman as she daintily patted the corner of her eye. *Maybe This Time* would give her new fans an emotional break. The stools around the piano were now filled and that woman was leading the singalong in her baritone voice.

The Bear took a quick break to chat with the people around the piano. "Not many can make the Queen of South Beach cry anymore. I'm Jacqueline, and this is Diego."

"So nice to meet you," she said. They became better acquainted through Sondheim, *Les Miserables*, and *Caberet*.

Jacqueline gave Judy a tour of the house and sat her next to Diego. She knew a family style brunch with a who's who of Miami Beach personalities would be a great networking opportunity.

"Does everyone know the Warsaw Anniversary Party is coming up soon?" Diego's question got everyone talking at the same time, confusing Judy. "Art of Seduction has the performance contract," looking at Judy. "When I heard you sing the other night, I came up with an idea that I'd like to run by you sometime. Have you been to the Warsaw Ballroom yet?"

She laughed. "Yet?"

"You would be performing for your largest audience...yet. And I'd like you to close the night." Everyone's mouths dropped, as Jacqueline topped off their Bellinis.

She held up her glass. "To The Bear, at the Warsaw Anniversary Party!" As the glasses clinked, Judy wondered what she was getting herself into.

"Jacqueline, can you bring Judy to rehearsal next week?" Diego asked. "Tuesday at three."

Judy nodded to Jacqueline. "We'll be there."

Jacqueline helped Judy out of the car as Diego waited at the front doors. "Welcome to Warsaw!" he said. "Come meet your fellow Seduction players. Some you know from brunch."

There is something eerily sad about a space without its lasers, music, and revelers. The stale smell and dimness caused by the windowless isolation from the outside gives Judy pause. But then Diego's enthusiasm is contagious.

She heard the front door close and a round-faced man with puppy eyes and a captivating smile approached. "Hello, you must be Judy. I'm David." He kissed her on both cheeks.

"I'm so happy to finally meet you, David."

The dancers, go-go boys, and drag queens had performed at Warsaw before, so Diego would need to give Judy a tour. "Judy, this is Nelson. Let's take a walk around the club. There is something I want you two to see."

They followed Diego. Judy looked down at Nelson and smiled, wondering what he had in mind

180

for them. As they walked away, the others thought they had never seen anything so bizarre.

"Oh no, no, no!" Judy looked at Diego as they approached the ten-foot, gigantic, gold-colored, fiberglass penis sculpture backstage. Nelson giggled.

"Have a seat, Judy." Diego takes her hand and helps lower her onto the penis.

"Oh, this is very comfortable!" she laughs.

Diego lifts Nelson up and places him onto Judy's lap. They hear the sound of heel on wood approaching. As they look toward the clicking and the curtain is pulled back, Jacqueline's approval is evident. Standing next to Diego, "I've seen some strange things in my life, but this is curiouser and curiouser!"

At that moment, they all realized what Diego wanted to accomplish. The connection between the four of them locked.

Becoming Alice, "But I don't want to go among mad people," Judy remarked.

As the Cat, "Oh, you can't help that," Jacqueline replied, "we're all mad here. I'm mad. You're mad."

"How do you know I'm mad?"

"You must be, or you wouldn't have come here." They all nod in agreement.

"Let's go out on the stage." Diego helps his two performers down from the penis. "My plan is to move the sculpture onto the bar." They look out at the expanse of the room. Diego continues, "David ends his night with *I Will Survive*. I've asked him to remove Gloria's vocals and you will own the night, Judy."

"OK Diego, I trust you," she says, still a little hesitant.

"We're going to meet with the others for a bit, why don't you two hang out and get to know each other," he said to Judy and Nelson, as he walked off the stage with Jacqueline.

"So how did Diego discover you, Nelson?"

"I'm here with Tomas, one of the dancers. We work together at a circus in Guatemala."

"No shit!"

"Tomas took one of Diego's dance classes at the University of Miami. How did he discover you?"

"I sing at the Magnum Lounge. Diego and Jacqueline sat at the piano bar one night. Jacqueline invited me to one of her brunches, and here I am!"

"Let's go sit by the bar, I saw some comfortable lounge chairs over there."

"That sounds good. We can watch some of the rehearsal." She wanted to ask what it was like to be him. To live his life in his body. Then she thought he must be wondering the same about her. So they sat, and just as the Caterpillar, she asked, "So Nelson, who are YOU? If you're going to be dancing on my lap, I need to know," she said, smiling.

"Well, if you remember from *Alice's Adventures*, it's a curious feeling being me.

182

Sometimes I'm the right size for going through the little door into the lovely garden. But most of the time I can't reach the key on the table and keep sliding on the legs." Judy laughed. "So who are YOU?"

"It's a curious feeling being me, too. Sometimes I say to myself, 'That's quite enough, I hope I shan't grow any more, what will become of me?' Remember when Alice wonders if she will ever be able to leave the room?"

"Oh yes, and I remember she almost wishes she never went down that rabbit-hole. Do you think we are in the middle of some kind of fairytale?"

"Well, I used to think fairytales never happened, but I'm not so sure now. Remember when Alice thought 'There ought to be a book written about me, that there ought!' when she grows up?"

Then Nelson remembers, "And she says, 'at least there's no room to grow up any more HERE!'" They both look around the Ballroom as Diego continues to choreograph the upcoming evening with the others.

Judy hears him say, "And you two will move him horizontally down the catwalk, like on a conveyor belt." She's glad that has nothing to do with her.

David was ready and offered an invitation. "Come on over to the DJ booth and we can try a few arrangements." The instrumental and a cappella stems for *I Will Survive* were each released on 12" vinyl. David wanted Judy to hear the a cappella first, a couple of times. She then tried singing to the instrumental stem. David couldn't believe what he was hearing. Judy had already made it hers, and it would just get better. The rehearsing on the stage and on top of the speakers stopped to listen. Jacqueline leaned against the bar and proudly smiled.

Driving back over the Causeway, crossing Biscayne Bay, Jacqueline was curious. "So what are your dreams? You know you are destined for better than the Magnum Lounge," she said.

"Honestly, I'm loving my life now. Not many get to perform in Key West and Miami." Then she thought a bit. "I do miss Anita and Provincetown though." And thought a bit more. "Do you want to come up for a drink?"

"I was going to invite myself up anyway, dear. I have a surprise for you." She grabbed a large garment bag from the back seat and began the tedious ascent up the back stairs.

"Welcome to my Magnum abode."

"Well, this is very comfy," Jacqueline said, as she watched Judy maneuver herself through the galley kitchen.

"Make yourself comfortable. Would you like a Kamikaze?"

"Oh yes, please. The classic disco sour cocktail!" Jacqueline unzipped the garment bag as Judy squeezed some lemons. "Diego got this for you to wear for the Party." She draped it over the wingback chair and thought it might look better after a few Kamikazes.

She finished squeezing the lemons and strained the juice and chilled the martini glasses with some ice cubes. She filled a shaker with ice, poured the lemon juice, some vodka and triple sec, and shook vigorously. Poured in the martini glasses, garnished with lemon slices, Judy delivered the sour cocktails without spilling a drop. And then studied the poufy costume. "What the fuck?" she jeered, as they took their first sips.

"It is a bit excessive."

"You think?"

"So back to our earlier conversation. What about those dreams? This might be your road less traveled. Remember when Alice is in Wonderland and didn't know which road to follow? She asks Mr. Rabbit which one to take."

"Sure I remember. Mr. Rabbit tells her it depends on where she would like to go!"

"Exactly."

"I would like to go to Broadway," Judy divulged her dream. "Want another Kamikaze?"

Judy figured if Nelson could wear a Batman costume, she could wear a knee-length puffed-sleeve dress with a pinafore worn over the top and ankle-strap shoes. If Anita could only see her as Alice. In the time she spent primping with the girls, she had never laughed so hard in her life. Wanda was covered in tampons. Kitty Meow wore a three-foot headdress. Daisy Deadpetals had huge red platform pumps. Connie Casserole's wig was adorned in silk butterflies. And Judy wore a knee-length puffed sleeve dress. When they heard Jaime wishing everyone a happy anniversary, they were ready for their performances.

Diego knocked on the dressing-room door and waited for that drag inflection, "Come in."

"Hello girls. Everyone all set?" He heard assurances all around. "This is for you, Judy," and handed her a box, gift-wrapped with bunnies and a white bow. "Open it, you don't want to be late!"

She ripped off the wrapping and pulled out a soft, stuffed, white rabbit. "For a very important date!" And gave him and the rabbit a hug, "Thank you so much!" She looked at the spectacled rabbit, wearing a bow-tie, waistcoat and pocket watch, looks over to the girls and said, "We are ready for Wonderland!"

Tomas and Joshua escort her through the crowd to the stepladder at the end of the bar. They wait until she signals a readiness to take the first challenging step up to that gigantic, gold-colored, fiberglass penis. "OK boys, let's do this!" and they jumped up on the bar and offered their assistance up each stair and onto the balls. Judy arranged the pinafore worn over her knee-length, puffed-sleeve dress and offered a smile down to Nelson.

The two-foot Batman was then lifted up onto the bar and crawled onto Alice's lap and whispered "Let's follow the White Rabbit," and gave her a kiss on the cheek as they both looked out onto the Ballroom. Madonna's breathless voice of want and need accompanied ballet dancers as they sensually flowed from the stage to their places on the metal walkway. The silhouetted, intersex couples gyrated to *Justify My Love*, as Nelson gyrated on The Bear's lap, much to her amusement.

Hours later, David holds his arm up and waits for Judy to signal her readiness for the flood light and the E7 arpeggio chord to be rolled up the piano and back down again. Diego, Jacqueline and Xavier, and Nelson look up at Judy, knowing she is about to deliver that message of personal strength and defiance. They will survive.

The house lights come on to a round of applause as Judy takes her bows. Tomas and Joshua escort her back to the dressing room, where Jacqueline and Diego were waiting with a bouquet of roses. "Yellow for joy and friendship, my dear."

"Oh, they are gorgeous! Thank you so much," they hugged and kissed, and then saw a man she didn't know in her dressing room.

"Remember I said you'd never know who would be here tonight?" Jacqueline said. "Well, let me introduce a good friend."

At that moment, through the Nederlander Organization, the Broadway League of Governors, and Broadway Cares/Equity Fights AIDS, Judy's dream would begin to come true. Then a knock on the door, and Nelson came in. "You must have dropped this," he said, and passed the soft, stuffed white rabbit to her.

NELSON

Nelson was born in the Dominican Republic with microcephalic osteodysplastic primordial dwarfism type II. As a child, Nelson was often sick. Never actually diagnosed with MOPDII, it was obvious from an early age his body was very different than the rest of the kids in his town. He loved baseball. Although he couldn't compete with the neighborhood players, his two brothers played catch and pitched to him when they could. The abnormal development of his hip joints and curvature of the spine restricted his physical activity.

But it was the combination of his appearance and voice that often shocked or amused people. His prominent nose, long face with full cheeks, and small jaw and teeth gave him a freakish look. Due to the narrowing of his voice box, his high-pitched, nasal voice added to the amusement. Despite his brothers' protection, as he entered adolescence, the teasing was relentless.

Everyday tasks were a challenge. Step stools and ladders were a necessity in the bathroom, kitchen and bedroom. Perspective from so low to the floor always made everything seem so nonsensical. As a child, his mother would read *Alicia en el Pais de las Maravillas* at bedtime. He would dream of the dream throughout his life. A curious Nelson always wanted to follow the White Rabbit. Sometimes waking feeling empowered and sometimes feeling terrified. Always willing to eat the cake or drink from the bottle, but he preferred the cake.

From the city of Puerto Plata, Nelson grew up in a culture of Merengue, Bachata, and baseball. He loved all three, but quickly discovered that people were interested in watching him dance. So interested, in fact, that some were willing to pay for the spectacle. Life was a little better now for his family, but his parents saw an opportunity in this curiosity about their son. Poverty tends to make people do desperate things. They started to charge admission to watch Nelson dance in their corrugated, tin roofed house. Sometimes the village kids would peek between the gaps of the single layer, palm-wood boards.

After one of his performances, an unknown man approached Nelson's parents. "Buenos dias. My name is Mario. You have a uniquely talented son. Would you be interested in him performing in front of larger audiences?"

"We are worried about so many people coming to our little house that we have been thinking about stopping this. But my son loves to sing and dance." She called Nelson over to join the conversation. "What did you have in mind?"

"I am from Las Aguilas Humanas and Hermanos Mazzini Circuses. I heard about your dancing,

191

Nelson, and I wanted to come see for myself. I think you could be our main attraction someday. Here is my card. Call me and we will bring you to one of our circuses and you can meet our performers."

Puerto Plata Carnival is celebrated every February and March. Enriched by African and Spanish cultural influences, the festivities entertain the people in the streets of the city. Parades of the devil and its deities in masks called Tainas, music and popular dances and other demonstrations of the arts brought the coastal town to life. Much of Carnival is about opposites or the upside down world, and was Nelson's favorite time of the year. He loved the anonymity of the mask.

That anonymity didn't last long. Each year the organizers of the carnival chose the King Momo, who received the keys and represents the city. The original King Momo was a tall, fat man, so it was a surprise when the two-foot Nelson was crowned. As the crown was placed upon his head, he thought about his *Alicia en el Pais de las Maravillas* dreams. At the end of the procession, there was cake waiting.

Now that Nelson was becoming a young man, his mother understood that it was time for her son to discover the world, outside of her protective bubble. She would always want to keep him safe from cruelty, but his curiosity would pull him away from her. On this Carnival's last night, Nelson and his mom sat on the boardwalk wall, looking out at the ocean. "Mijo, it is almost time for you to leave us. I want to share you with the world," as she wrapped her arm around him and kissed him on his forehead. "I will call Mario and arrange for you to spend some time at Las Aguilas Humanas, if that is what you want."

Looking up into his mom's eyes, and with that classic Nelson smile, "I've been dreaming about the circus since Mario came to visit us. It's like Alice eating the mushroom!"

Surprised by the comparison, "Just make sure you eat from the right side." As she tickled her son's side, they both laughed. She was very good at hiding her many years of concern and worry, beginning early in Nelson's childhood. Boston Children's Hospital had become their home away from home.

Nelson's hip dislocation and worsening coxa vara required surgery. Through the help from Little People of America and Children's Hospital, this first trip to Boston, and others to follow, would be provided at no cost to his family. The swan boats in Boston Common, the giant's room at the Children's Museum, and a warm summer's night at Fenway Park were his favorite things to do through his often painful physical therapy. So he worked through it because he knew it was necessary if he was to continue dancing.

The history of the circus for little people goes back to medieval court entertainment. The first standup comedians, with kings and queens as the audience, could get away with saying things that others couldn't. These jesters became advisors and an important form of entertainment. This eventually led to circuses as one of the only way little people could earn a living.

So as Nelson's mom waved goodbye as he boarded the plane to Guatemala, she worried about her boy's health, safety, and happiness. One of the most violent countries in the world, and also one where poverty and inequality are everywhere, he would travel with Las Aguilas Humanas for three months. At least that was the plan. All his possessions in one easy to carry backpack, she made sure he had his copy of *Alicia en el Pais de las Maravillas*.

Mario met him at the airport. "I'm so excited you are here with us. My family can't wait to meet you!"

Nelson stood on the passenger seat of the pickup truck so he could see this new country. It looked like home until they turned into an open field and parking lot. He called it the front yard. Then he saw what looked like a small town, only almost everything was on wheels. And if it wasn't on wheels it was a tent.

Mario could see that Nelson was tired, so he took his backpack and helped him out of the truck. He looked around at the organized movement of everyone doing their jobs. The sounds of hammering, the yelling of frantic orders, the barking of dogs, and lion roars coming from a prison-like trailer, while he tried to adjust to the sun-bright whiteness of the tents, it all seemed overwhelming.

He followed Mario through the back yard. Although he tried, he couldn't keep up with all the names he heard in greetings. "Capacity tonight! Might have to spread some straw on the ground for people to sit on." The smells were too much of a distraction. Perfume, soap, paint, barbequed meat, animal waste, and truck exhaust were all in preparation for the evening's straw house.

"Flags up!"

Nelson looked at Mario confused. "Ah, perfect timing. You hungry?" He nodded and smiled. "This is the cook house. I'll introduce you to everyone and then we'll eat."

They entered the tent and Nelson wondered what the circus was celebrating. He had never seen so much food, except for carnival and weddings. They joined Mario's family at their table and there was a special chair for him so he could sit at the same height as the others.

"Please everyone, may I have your attention! I would like to introduce all of you to the newest member of our family, Nelson." Everyone applauded and Nelson waved. "He will be joining us for three months. You have all been working very hard preparing for tonight's show, so enjoy the food and when you get a chance, introduce yourself to Nelson."

The waiters got back to work. Trays of tamales were served. A choice of tamales negros or chichitos today. Black tamales are darker and sweeter than red because of the chocolate, raisins, prunes and almonds. Chuchitos are almost always offered. They are wrapped in dried corn husks, with a simple tomato salsa and sprinkled with a hard, salty white cheese.

Although not a Dominican staple, Nelson appreciated the hours of work in preparing Guatemalan tamales. Typically wrapped in plantain leaves or maxan leaves, they use cooked masa. As a special welcome, the cook house staff baked a bizcocho Dominicano for Nelson. This cake was always for a Dominican family celebration. With a meringue frosting, they somehow knew his favorite filling was guava.

Nelson was sitting next to Mario's son, Tomas. Because they were the same age, he decided they would share a room and Tomas would teach him about circus life. Actually, in time, they would teach each other about life. But for now, they had to learn to like each other.

"Bring Nelson to your room and help him get settled. Try not to get into any trouble before the show." He gave his son an all-too-familiar look.

"I wish! I have too much work to do to get into any trouble."

"Yeah, I've heard that before, mi hijo," as he gave him a kiss on his forehead, and a gentle smack on his face.

Their room had wheels. A bunk bed and two lockers, but no ladder. "You get the top bunk."

"You know that's impossible."

"You're in the fucking circus my friend. Nothing is impossible!" And he picked him up and threw him into his bed. "Comfortable?"

They lay in their bunks and Tomas asks, "So why are you here?"

"Look at me. You know why I'm here. Why are you here?"

Tomas received a Bachelor of Business Administration from the University of Miami in Coral Gables. He often wonders why he is here. Nelson is the first person ever to ask him that question.

"There are a lot of people counting on my dad and me to make this business a success. You saw everyone today. This is a hard life, but it's in my blood. And sometimes I escape to my other life."

"Oh?"

197

"You ever been to the US?"

"Boston a few times."

"Maybe sometime I'll show you Miami. Crazy beautiful there!"

"Maybe show me your other life?"

"We all have other lives, don't we?" Tomas smiled. "Let's head over to clown alley before the speck. I want you to meet a few people."

The alley reminded Nelson of Carnival preparation. Perhaps Tomas thought his training should begin here, as a clown. They walked over to three clowns. "Meet Hector, Juan, and Anna. I need to go get ready. You three take good care of our new friend until Mario comes to get him."

"We will," Hector assures Tomas.

"It's great to meet the King Momo!" Anna said. "Mario has told us a lot about you. Ah, here he comes now."

"Hello everyone. How was your afternoon, Nelson? I hope Tomas helped you get settled."

"He did, Señor. He went to get ready for tonight."

Anna looked at Hector and Juan for approval. "I have a question, Mario. Would it be OK if Nelson came with us to the training session tomorrow?" The two nodded their heads and waited for a response.

He looked at Nelson. "Oh, I don't know about that. I'll talk to you tonight, OK? Let's go inside and watch the show."

Nelson was so excited it was hard for Mario to think of him as a young man. The floss that he bought him was almost as big as he was. The music signaled the beginning of the spectacle. As *Fanfara Nunziale* played, the grand entrance of clowns, acrobats, jugglers, unicyclists, and trained animals brought out the child in everyone in the house. Mario pointed to the clowns and asked, "Do you want to become a Joey?"

Nelson was quickly learning the circus lingo and slang and assumed he was being asked if he wanted to become a clown. "I do, very much! Clowns make people happy!"

That was the answer Mario was hoping he would hear. "OK, you should go to the City tomorrow with the others. Anna will watch over you and bring you back safe."

The next day, Nelson, Anna and the other Las Aguilas Humanas clowns joined some one hundred fifty smiling clowns as they paraded down Paseo de La Sexta. The United Urban Clowns of Guatemala gathered to publicly demand that their profession be respected as an art. The parade continued to their hotel, where Nelson would participate in his first training session for beginners in the art of clowning.

Anna gathered everyone in the lobby. "Let's all meet here at 8 o'clock and we will go out to dinner. Enjoy your sessions."

At Nelson's first session, he learned about the code of conduct for clowns. There are eight clown commandments, most of which he thought he could abide by, especially the ones about clown standards of makeup and costuming. There was one about not drinking alcoholic beverages while in makeup or clown costume he wasn't sure about. Nelson had to memorize these commandments and do some reading on the art of clowning before the next session, and hoped Anna would help him after dinner.

The clown alley walked to Kacao, a popular restaurant known for the national dishes of jocon, pepian, and tamales. Nelson was excited to hear the live marimba music. "Order what you want everyone. This is on Mario, buen provecho!" Anna looks at Nelson. "I would highly recommend the pepian."

Served piping hot in a stone bowl, Nelson took his first taste of the thick, smoky chunks of meat. The stew of roasted spices, beef, vegetables and fruits was served with rice and freshly made corn tortillas. "This is so delicious!" Nelson announced to the table, and everyone raised their bottles. "Thank you everyone for inviting me!"

Nelson started his third bottle of Gallo. The beer was perfect with the recardos and he was bastante borracho! Anna was sitting next to him. She leaned over and whispered, "Don't worry, I told Diego I would take good care of you." She caressed his thigh under the table.

At first, Anna kept her eyes closed. They kissed each other cautiously, both still wondering if this should happen. She took his head into her hands and moved him onto her neck. She shuddered as the tip of his tongue gently licked up and down her neck. He pulled back her chocolate brown, shoulder length hair, continuing to kiss near her ear, he softly blew onto the damp line, causing another shudder.

She felt a strength in his movement unlike other men three times his size. Surprised by his confidence, he held up his index finger to signal a quick interruption and looked into her eyes for approval. Nelson hopped off the bed and returned with the ice bucket and a blindfold.

He licked and kissed her cleavage and moved from breast to breast with a light fingertip caress. Blindfolded, Anna moaned when he cupped his hand over one breast, rest her nipple between his thumb and index finger and squeezed. With an ice cube in his mouth, he licked her areola and finally her nipple. As his mouth moved to her other breast, the chill from the ice was something she had never experienced.

"Esto parece buena?" he whispered in her ear.

"Esto se siente incredible!" she moaned again.

A knock on the door woke both of them up. "Anna, we are going downstairs for breakfast. Should I wake Nelson?"

"No, I'll wake him. We'll be down soon." He giggled and she put her hand over his mouth. She then replaced her hand with her mouth. They quickly kissed. "OK, you need to go to your room and get ready. I'll see you in the restaurant." Nelson got dressed, slowly opened the door to make sure no one was out in the hall, and went back to his room to take a shower.

He was confused, excited, and exhausted. He dragged the chair into the bathroom so he could reach the sink. Nelson looked at himself in the mirror and remembered something his mother once told him. "Hijo de mi alma, we all have a soulmate." But he didn't want to talk to his mother about this. He wanted to talk to Tomas.

Surprised, Anna kissed him in front of the others when he arrived at breakfast. "Hope you're hungry. I ordered for us." One minute later a huge plate of steak, longaniza, fried plantains, eggs, black beans, crema and tortillas arrived. "These are paches, tamales filled with pork and potato."

"Wow, this is so much food!" Nelson didn't usually have a large breakfast.

"Eat up everyone. Remember, after our final sessions we have to get back to Las Aguilas for a matinee," Anna announced.

Nelson had some decisions to make. What kind of clown did the alley need? What type of clown fit his personality? At his session, they explored the Whiteface and Auguste clown types, as well as the tramp and character clowns. The Whiteface clown has decent manners and often bosses the other clowns around. The Auguste clown is eager to please. Anna would probably think of him as an Auguste clown.

Nelson can certainly do clumsiness. He can also be a troublemaker, using slapstick to get away with his pranks. He is more innocent than unintelligent. So is he a joker or a fool? Or both.

One thing he learned, he needed a plan. A name, carefully chosen. A face, artfully drawn. A costume, appropriately sized. A prop, to enhance the persona. And most importantly, a written skit, rehearsed. Anna would have to help with that. And finally, he was sure they would have to get Mario's approval.

He was so excited to see Tomas back in their room on wheels. Where to begin? He didn't want to be one of those guys always talking about sex. He couldn't even if he wanted to. But damn, he had so many questions!

"Welcome back my little friend! So what did you think of the City?"

"I loved it. The parade of clowns was amazing. The hotel was nice. Great food. Learned a lot in my sessions."

"Oh yeah? Well that all sounds very boring to me." He could tell Nelson was holding something from him.

"Well, I did get drunk. Oh yeah, and I had sex with Anna," he said, like it was no big deal.

"Dios mio!"

"Lo se! Que hago ahora?" he asked.

"How the fuck do I know?" Tomas laughed. Surprised by the question, he asked back, "What do you want to do?"

"I like Anna. I want to have some fun while I'm here learning about circus life. And I hope she wants to have fun with me."

"I've known Anna for a long time. I can promise you, if she slept with you, she likes you, too. Just goes to show you, there is someone for everyone in this life."

"That's what my mother always told me. I never believed her until now."

Mario knocked on the door and came in. "Welcome back Nelson. Did you have fun at the conference?" Nelson looked at Tomas with that "don't you dare" look.

"I did, Señor. I need to get some advice from you about becoming a clown. I don't know what to do next."

"OK, we can talk about it during dinner and tonight's show. Until then, why don't you take Nelson to see all our animals?" Tomas nodded. "I'll see you in the cook house."

A strange feeling of anxiousness came over Nelson at the thought of being near some of the animals he had been hearing since he arrived. Watching the animal acts safely up in the audience was amazing. The big cats, elephants, horses, and bears obediently performed with grace and precision. He wanted to see the birds, sea lions, and the domestic cats and dogs up close, not so much the others.

Of course, Tomas wanted to show him the tigers first. As they got closer to the cages, Nelson could feel himself physically shaking. There was a Bengal in one cage and a Sumatran in the other. Both seemed like they wanted to rip Nelson into bite size pieces, or so he thought.

The four Asian elephants were grouped together with their trainer. "Nelson, this is Jose." He waved from a safe distance, not as afraid of the elephants as he was of Jose with his bull-hook. The chained elephants had a sadness in their eyes.

"We are very proud of our stallions and geldings," Tomas said. "Our performing horses steal the show. Come meet Maria." He started to feel afraid again. He didn't like being near horses. Their size and strength overwhelmed him.

"Hello boys," Maria said from atop one of the stallions.

"How's everything going Maria? This is Nelson. I'm showing him around."

"Glad to meet you Nelson. Patience, understanding, and lots of carrots today," she said to Tomas, laughing. "I'll bring you for a ride sometime, if you want Nelson."

"OK, bye," he said, hoping it wasn't anytime soon.

"Come see our newest arrival," Tomas reassured Nelson he would like this. They could hear the squeals of mild distress followed by cooing sounds as they approached the small cage. Inside was a black bear cub, tethered to a hook in the ground by a short rope.

"Why is he alone?" asked Nelson. "Where is his mother?"

"I have no idea. We should ask Mario." Tomas thought a minute, "I'm sure they will start training him soon." Nelson wondered if the only difference between him and the cub was the cage.

Looking frustrated, Tomas said, "OK, come with me. I have a surprise for you."

They entered a fenced-in circular area and Nelson was suddenly jumped on and then knocked to the ground. He began to laugh as his face was being covered with the saliva of five yellow

Labrador puppies. "Ok my friend, I'm going to leave you with them while I go check on a few things." Nelson was trying to listen as he was being attacked. "Pick the one you like the most. He's yours."

"Really?" All his life he had wanted a dog.

"Really. I'll be right back."

Nelson continued to roll around as the puppies playfully jumped all over him. He then sat up, folded his legs, and patted each one. It didn't take long for their personalities to show. Strangely, one kept looking him in his eyes, seeming to connect in a way the others weren't. This little guy sat in front of him. Nelson held out his hand and he offered his paw as if to signal a done deal. And then he curled up on his lap.

"That was quick," Tomas said. "I got a collar and leash for him. Make sure he pees before you bring him inside."

Nelson and his puppy bonded from the moment they met. Now he had two names to find. One that fit his clown identity and another for his new best friend. Some were already calling him King or Momo or King Momo. The puppy had a regal prance while walking on his leash, so he thought King would be perfect. And he could be Momo, Momo the Clown. This was the beginning of his act and he couldn't wait to tell Anna.

King jumped on everyone at clown alley, tail wagging, happily greeting each of Nelson's new friends. They both gave Anna a kiss. King's was sloppier. "Everyone, this is King," Nelson said.

"Oh my god, he is so cute!" Anna said, wiping the dog saliva off her face.

"I'm going to bring him back to play with his brothers and sisters while we eat dinner."

"That's a good idea. I'll see you at the cook house."

Nelson sat with Mario during that evening's show. So much had happened to him since the last show. Did he need permission or was he seeking approval? He now watched again as the music signaled the beginning of the spectacle. As *Fanfara Nunziale* played, the grand entrance of clowns, acrobats, jugglers, unicyclists, and trained animals brought out the child in everyone in the house. But this time was different. Mario looked over at him and realized that Nelson was now one of the family.

"I hear you have a puppy," he said, expecting an explanation.

"Si, señor. His name is King. I have a plan that I would like to discuss with you." Mario looked surprised. "I would like to partner with Anna for an act that includes King."

"You know, most of our dog acts have always been with poodles, but I'll give you and Anna some time to work with King. Let's see how he does." They both saw the cues given, and the clowns left the alley and entered the big top. As they began their skits, Mario said with a smile, "I hear you like Anna."

"Si, quiero."

The next morning, Tomas and Nelson were outside playing with King. He would endlessly fetch the ball, patiently waiting for it to be thrown. "Remember I told you I wanted to show you Miami, my other life?" Tomas asked. "Would you like to come with me next month?"

Always willing to follow the White Rabbit, Nelson knew this would be an adventure. So, of course, he said yes, but with reservations. What about King, and Anna, and rehearsals, and money. They would have a month to work out the details, and in that time he hoped Tomas would come to realize that it could sometimes be difficult to be his friend. Just as it was sometimes difficult to be his son or brother.

"Of course, I would love to! But who will take care of King?"

"You'll have to talk to Anna about that, I guess."

"Si, I'll see her at breakfast. I have a lot to talk to her about. Vamos, tengo hambre."

Nelson loved breakfast at the cook house. His favorite tamales with fried plantains, eggs and longaniza, black beans, steak, tortillas, and coffee with crema would begin a very busy day. With a full plate, he sat in his usual accommodated chair next to Anna.

"I heard you were going to Miami with Tomas," Anna said matter-of-factly.

Nelson used the time chewing the garlicky sausage and egg to carefully respond to Anna's inquiry. He was surprised she knew, so this delay tactic gave him some time to think. With Tomas away from the table, and knowing it would not be possible, "Why don't you come with us?"

Entertained by what she thought was Nelson's ignorance, she laughed. "My little world traveler! Must be nice to be able to afford such a carefree life."

Ignoring the sarcasm, "Can you come to our room after breakfast? I have some ideas I need to talk to you about."

"Sure, I have some time." As Tomas joined them with a full plate, he received a glaring look from Anna. "You'll be joining us, too."

"What the hell did I do now?" He knew.

Back at the trailer, Nelson took control of the conversation. With King at his feet, Nelson first needed Tomas and Anna to realize that he was going to fully take advantage of the outsiders' curiosity concerning his smallness. This not only involved his circus performances but traveling for public appearances. He wondered if Tomas could help in marketing his brand?

Mario was aware of Nelson's many health issues. It was time to share these concerns with the two people that he would be spending most of his time.

And finally, time. Nelson asked if Anna would want to be part of the act with King. If yes, when would the act be ready? Nelson asked Tomas how long would they be in Miami? How much money would he need? Would Anna take care of King while he was away? They talked for hours about the next month.

Joshua met them at Miami International. Tomas had talked about Joshua so much, Nelson felt like he already knew him. And as they traveled over the MacArthur Causeway onto Miami Beach, he watched as contentment overtook Tomas. His friend had returned to his other life, and he was honored to be welcomed into it.

Down 5th Street onto Ocean Drive, Nelson tried to keep up with the passing Art Deco buildings. Down 14th Street onto Collins Ave, he tried to keep up with the passing scantily clad beautiful people. Stopped at the intersection of Collins and Española Way, Joshua said "That's where we'll be tonight!" When they turned left onto Española, Nelson saw the pastel blue Warsaw Ballroom sign passing by. "Diego will be happy to see you again."

"Are we dancing tonight?"

"We sure are! Let's give Nelson the full SoBe experience on his first night."

"Oh, I don't think my little friend could take that. We might have to spread it out over the weekend." Tomas poked him in his side.

"Bring it on!" Nelson challenged. "I can keep up with you two anytime." Tomas was beginning to think he was right, but he knew they still needed to be careful. Sometimes Tomas had watched Nelson take his meds, but he didn't know what they were for, and he was pretty sure he wasn't supposed to drink. Nelson liked to drink and Tomas certainly understood why.

Joshua had just moved into a small, one bedroom apartment on Meridian Ave. When they arrived they decided to take a nap. Nelson was tired and would sleep on the couch. Tomas was tired too, but didn't get much sleep. When Nelson woke, he was alone in the apartment because the go-go boys needed a quick workout at Jeremiah's. This would give him some time to check out the accessibility.

Joshua's empathy of Nelson's everyday struggles was evident as he looked around at the stepstools in the kitchen and bathroom. There was even a smaller one in the living room so he could sit at the coffee table to eat. Many items had been moved to lower cabinets which reduced the climbing he would have had to do. Nelson had learned to adjust to most obstacles, and he was very grateful to Joshua for reducing many of them.

Unfamiliar bathrooms always made Nelson feel uneasy, so he thought he might as well conquer that first. Two of Nelson's biggest fears were falling and getting burned, and both possibilities were in bathrooms and kitchens. He would take a shower before Joshua and Tomas got back to save time before going out. He climbed into the tub and saw the faucet was clearly labeled hot and cold with arrows, but he always tested the water temperature anyway. He had learned the hard way to start cold and gradually add the hot. While drying himself, he heard Joshua and Tomas come home and was relieved. He didn't like being alone.

Joshua and Tomas brought Cuban food home with them. A spicy mojo chicken with warm mango avocado salsa, black beans and rice, Cuban baby-back ribs, and flan was a perfect welcome to South Beach.

Joshua made some strong Café Bustelo which paired perfectly with the rich creamy custard. "Did you know that Nelson is in the Guinness Book of Records?" Tomas informed Joshua, although Nelson never really remembered that happening. Mario seemed to think it happened, so he went with it.

"We will have to mention that when we introduce you to Diego tonight. The anniversary party is soon. He might want to put you in the show."

213

"You know, when Mario came to my house, my parents were making some pretty good money charging to see my performances." Nelson was thinking out loud. "People are curious about anything different. We've talked about this, Tomas." Coffee and dessert were finished, beers were opened.

"Yes, I remember, with Anna. It might be time for you to take on an agent."

Nelson trusted Tomas to act in his best interest. "Is that something you would want to do?"

"Of course I'll be your agent!" Tomas felt honored and challenged. "After Warsaw tonight, we can talk about what that might mean, OK?" Finishing his beer, "Let's get ready!"

Nelson thought he was pretty much already ready. He didn't own any club attire. He had never been in a club. So he waited for Tomas and Joshua to get ready. They would walk to the club in their jeans and Timberlands, but the gym bag contained the gear for the night's performances. A variety of boxer, classic, and bikini briefs, and some booty shorts nicely displayed their hard work at Jeremiah's. Finally, some extra-long socks to stuff the tips into, and they were ready.

Joshua and Tomas were both 6' 2" tall. Nelson was 2' 2" short, so he had to take at least three times as many steps for their one. This would exhaust his friend so, once outside the apartment, Tomas got down on one knee and Nelson climbed onto his back and sat on the shoulder of a giant.

The ride to Warsaw gave Nelson a view rarely experienced. He could see over hedges into yards and windows, faces were easier to see as they drove and walked by, dogs weren't scary, and the stars were within reach. He had eaten from the right side of the mushroom.

Nelson had grown accustomed to people's reaction to him. From his perch atop Tomas, the looks weren't the usual disbelief, but of anticipation. The club line watched as the three met the approval of Jaime. Welcoming them with an open pull on the door, the tease of another wave of deep tribal base reminded the future patrons that the wait would be worth it. Tomas kept Nelson on his shoulders for the introduction to Jacqueline and then backed up to the bar. Nelson slid off and stood atop his newfound claim. Diego was watching and planning.

Tomas needed to leave Nelson in good hands while they performed. Scott worked at the gym and at this end of the bar. "Scott, this is Nelson. Nelson meet Scott. You need anything, he will take good care of you." The two shook hands as Tomas and Joshua went to get undressed. Diego smiled from a distance.

"So what can I get you, Nelson?"

"Corona please"

"Sure, be right back."

He sat on the bar, with his feet dangling, looking out at the dancefloor. He took a few gulps of the cold beer, and wondered if he dared to dance. As if reading his mind, Diego came over to introduce himself and asked, "Do you want to get out there?"

"I'd love to, but was going to wait for Tomas and Joshua."

"That's not necessary." Diego signaled to a couple of his friends. One carried him to the floor and they danced until he was happily exhausted, and then returned him safely to the bar. Diego was waiting. "Nelson, would you be interested in performing in the Anniversary Party next month?"

"Sure, if the money's right!" He took a few long gulps of his beer. "Tomas is my manager." Diego looked surprised and impressed.

"Great! If I can work everything out with him, we will be having a rehearsal soon. Hope to see you then. I'll be over at the DJ booth if you need me." They hugged. Those in the SoBe club loop watched, assuming this was anniversary related, and suddenly realized they weren't in the loop as much as they thought.

Tomas, Joshua, and Nelson arrived at the corner of Collins and Española Way and entered Warsaw. They headed toward the sound of voices, easy to do in the empty club. Nelson was unaccustomed to his line of sight being unobstructed, looking around as if it was his first time. He thought about how humiliating it was to sometimes be carried from the bar to the dance floor and back. He wondered how much humiliation would be involved with this next gig. He was soon to find out. "Hi everyone, I'd like you to meet Nelson," Diego said. "Nelson, this is Kitty Meow, Wanda, Connie Casserole, and Daisy Deadpetals." He thought about his circus experiences, and then Jacqueline and Judy joined them!

"Judy, this is Nelson. Let's take a walk around the club. There is something I want you two to see."

They followed Diego backstage, looking at each other uncomfortably. Nelson gazed at the enormous, golden phallic sculpture and giggled. When Diego helped Judy up onto the balls, its purpose became evident to him.

As Diego placed him onto Judy's lap, Jacqueline pulls the curtain back and joins the absurdity. At that moment, they all realized what Diego wanted to accomplish, and they would try their best to make it happen.

They wanted to make an Anniversary entrance. So Nelson decided he would put on the Batman costume at the apartment. Out on the sidewalk, Tomas got down on one knee and Nelson climbed onto his back. That ride to Warsaw had become routine. The hiding behind the mask and cape flapping behind them was not, and again he had eaten from the right side of the mushroom. Onto Española Way, the unusually long club line watched as the three performers disappeared into the club. On the way to their dressing room, with the house lights still on, they waved hello to Jacqueline and David in their booths. They heard laughter coming from the girls' dressing room. Everyone needed some preparation time.

He watched Tomas and Joshua change out of their jeans and into their booty shorts. For perfectly sculpted bodies, never perfect enough, preparation time involved pushups. Nelson had never done a pushup in his life. Dancing was his cardio, and he would get plenty of that tonight, as the house lights dimmed. Jamie yelled out to the bartenders, barbacks, drag queens, go-go boys, Jacqueline and Diego, "Happy Anniversary everyone!" and opened the front doors.

Tomas and Joshua danced a while before it was time for Nelson to perform. They escorted Judy through the crowd to the bar, where he was already waiting. They jumped on top of the bar and helped Judy up onto the balls of the penis. Nelson then crawled onto her lap and whispered "Let's follow the White Rabbit." When Nelson gave her a kiss on the cheek, David looked over at them, waved, and began his *White Rabbit* extended mix.

They take a break from the penis while Cher promises to give the crowd the stars flickering above the dancefloor. Nelson watches as the Art of Seduction dancers, dressed as sailors, escort the drag Cher as she sings about turning back time. He wonders how Anna and King are doing. After the show, another marathon set is launched. Joshua places him near his platform to dance to the repetitive four on the floor, where he could keep an eye on him.

He rejoins The Bear a few more times until her solo moment. His friends sit him on the bar as the white flood hits Judy, and she begins to sing Gloria Gaynor's *I Will Survive*. He looks over at Diego, and as their eyes meet, they both nod, signaling a recognition of this woman's talent and the message of defiance and survival shared by the Warsaw community.

DIEGO

Flamenco created the roots Diego longed for in his life. The North End of Boston provided a connection to his Italian father, the South End to his Spanish Roma mother. His Rom ethnicity seemed to provide a misguided justification for his childhood nomadic foster care. The Commonwealth decided his thirteen-year-old mother could not provide the care needed, so the pattern of mistrust and self-defense was established early.

The mother church of the Archdiocese of Boston was home during a part of his childhood. In the rectory behind the Cathedral, his bedroom was spartan and musty. The South End neighborhood of beautiful brownstones could be dangerous. So Maria, the rectory cook, walked him to and from grammar school every day. She tried to protect him from a world of predators, both inside and out.

Maria read to him every night. Their favorite books were *Alice's Adventures in Wonderland* and *Through the Looking Glass*. Every time, Maria would act like it was the first time she had read the stories, always wondering about the locked doors and whether she could be as brave as Alice.

The secrets behind those locked doors, also protected, but under a powerful seal of evil dogma, would haunt Diego subconsciously, influencing his every life decision.

Voted prom king of his East Boston High School graduating class, he still needed the escape and discipline the US Marines would offer. Starting with boot camp, the months of hard physical challenge paid off. He looked amazing in his blue dress uniform. Fluent in English, Spanish, Italian, Portuguese, and American Sign, Diego quickly became a VIP escort and interpreter. He was proud to represent his adopted country to royalty and dignitaries from around the world.

To understand flamenco helps to understand Diego. A mix of cultures, the deep song started as a passionate cry of despair of the poor and marginalized Andalusian peasants. The guitar, along with the dancer, carries a message touching the deepest of human emotions. The passion, anger and heartache of Diego's life shows in his face as he dances. Sometimes his expression turns to pride as he achieves near perfection from hours of practice. A master of the cante jondo style of singing, Carmen Linares provided his motivation for that perfection. Diego's neighbors often heard her forceful voice in *Escandalo* as he danced on the hardwood floors.

For all the obvious reasons, it was hard for Diego to settle in one place for long. After the Marines, he had returned to Boston, and did settle into a regular routine for a while. Out every night with his best friend Javier, sleeping in late, an odd job here and there, and flamenco practice as much as possible.

Time proved Boston to be too small. Diego had developed a very impressive resume from which he could pursue his need to travel. As a flight attendant, Trans World Airlines provided the opportunity for him to keep on moving. Bidding route assignments and travel benefits brought him to London, Madrid, Paris, Buenos Aires, Mexico City, San Juan, and Miami.

He attended the annual Flamenco Festival in London at Sadler's Wells. From puro to contemporary, the dance venue hosted two weeks of unique shows.

He was able to spend a few months with a renowned Flamenco teacher in Madrid, where he was able to perform at a tapas bar with the flamenco guitarist Antonia Jimenez. Female flamenco guitarists are a tiny, uncelebrated minority. There are not many *tocaoras* accompanying *cante* and *baile*, and they became quick friends.

He participated in a three day festival of singing and dancing at the Grande Halle de la Villette in Paris. Internationally known performers shared their knowledge of the art of flamenco, including Gitanas Andaluzas and the Belen Maya Company.

He often stayed in the central part of Buenos Aires where he frequented an underground flamenco venue called Cantares. Diego was most content with some belly-warming locro and a bottle of oak Cabernet Sauvignon. This hearty stew of corn, beans, pork, pancetta, carrots, squash, and potatoes always made him feel welcome.

He saw some of the greatest flamenco artists perform in the tablaos of Mexico City. One night, his friend, Jorge, an eclectic and talented guitarist, accompanied Mercedes Amaya in a fearless dance he would never forget.

He had a favorite tablao in old San Juan. Barrachina had the best shrimp mofongo and whole red snapper. He had to get their famous piña colada while watching the flamenco shows.

But he found the true taste and feel of Spain in Calle Ocho, Miami. In the "City Beautiful" Coral Gables, CAVA Tablao Flamenco and Restaurant was the real deal. Authentic Andalusian food and flamenco *puro* shows connected his heart to this place. Home to the University of Miami, the city's architectural style is almost entirely Mediterranean Revival. Its old-fashioned, tree-lined boulevards and numerous shopping boutiques and restaurants have made Coral Gables a popular destination. Only thirty minutes from Miami Beach, Diego would make it his new home.

Diego was nervous about his TWA future. When home, while having his morning coffee, he would quickly browse the Miami Herald Help Wanted section. He circled anything that looked interesting and grabbed the scissors. The School of Music at the University of Miami was looking for a dance instructor.

He began teaching classes in movement skills and dance forms from various cultures. Transition always brings opportunity. TWA was in transition. South Beach was in transition. The LGBT community was in transition. Diego saw the opportunity. His flight attendant days were over. The Art of Seduction was incorporated.

There were twelve students in his World History of Dance course. They would explore their own lives and cultures through dance. On this first day, Diego knew he would have to encourage these students to take risks and share. Who were they? Could they express their own histories through dance? They would not be reading about the history of dance and writing a paper in this class. And four would become life-long friends, each dancing through life in their own way, along with Diego.

"Hello everyone, please call me Diego. I am a flamenco dancer from Boston. During our time together, my role will be to choreograph your histories. So, what risks are you willing to take? Who are you? Through dance, how will you share

225

with us those answers? Take a minute to think, and when you're ready, let's get to know each other." Surprised at the exercise, the students thought a while, some wrote notes.

"Hola, my name is Tomas. I am a circus performer from Guatemala. Through my dance, I hope I can express the thrill and danger of gravity on the trapeze."

"Hello everyone, my name is Jacqueline. I am a drag queen from Boston. Through my dance, I want to share the risky transformation of my daily life."

"Hey there, my name is Joshua. I am a football player from Salt Lake City. Through my dance, I will share how I move through life without getting tackled."

"Hello, my name is Becky. I am a bartender from Toronto. Through my dance, I want to show the graceful movements of creating a mind-altering concoction."

As the introductions continued, Diego realized how much they would all learn from each other in the weeks ahead. He was also thinking about the Art of Seduction and his vision of offering his clients something they had never seen before. Some of his performers were sitting right in front of him.

During the next few weeks, Tomas and Joshua became friends and often rehearsed together at the Ring Theatre on campus. Built in 1951, the building's circular design placed the audience in a "ring" around the stage. In the 1970s, the Ring changed to a three-sided thrust. Diego's students would be performing their life dances at the Ring, giving an emotional, intimate connection to their invited guests. Unbeknownst to Tomas and Joshua, it would also be an audition.

As the semester was coming to an end, Diego wanted his students to share their music and video choices. It was time to share their histories.

Tomas chose *The Carnival is Over* by Dead Can Dance, an experimental darkwave band from Australia. The video contains performers dressed as jesters, animals in circus decorations, a fire eater, a man flapping his ears, tightrope walkers, and clowns.

Joshua chose *Simply the Best* by Tina Turner. His video begins with aerial views of the Salt Lake Temple spires, closing in on the All Seeing Eyes on each of the center towers. The Eye watches as he sprints to the right, off to the races into the end zone. Again, the Eye watches a one-handed, super stretch touchdown.

Jacqueline chose *Do Ya Wanna Funk* by Sylvester. It made sense that the "Queen of South Beach" would choose the "Queen of Disco".

Becky chose *I Still Haven't Found What I'm Looking For* by U2. Maybe because she had spoken with the tongue of angels and had held the hand of a devil.

As the Theatre was emptying, Diego hugged his four new friends, "Let's celebrate! I'd like to take you to La Taberna Giralda for some paella. The best I've ever had, it's cooked over a wood-burning fire."

"That sounds wonderful. The sangria is on me!" Jacqueline announced.

"Before the show I was so nervous I couldn't eat, but I'm starving now!" Joshua said as he put his arm around Tomas.

Arriving at the classic taberna, they ordered two pitchers. The sangria had sat overnight, waiting. A traditional recipe of bright Rioja, simple syrup, oranges, lemon, peaches, and cinnamon stick is poured over frozen fruit. "To Diego! Thanks for an amazing experience. We learned a lot about ourselves this semester." Joshua raised his glass with the others.

"I want to thank all of you, too. And I also want you to know there was another reason I invited you here." They all looked puzzled and leaned in. "Not too long ago I started an entertainment company called The Art of Seduction. One of my clients has become the Copa in Key West. Joshua and Tomas, I would like you to dance at the club." They both looked at each other and smiled.

"I've always wanted to see Key West!" Tomas said.

"Becky, there is an amazing bar in the club balcony. How would you like to bartend there?"

"Bartending in Key West? Fuck yeah!"

"Jacqueline, I would like you to be my Mistress of Ceremonies and also work the ticket booth."

"I love the Copa, and as Becky put it so succinctly, fuck yeah!" She raised her glass of sangria, "To the Art of Seduction!"

A large, wide, round, shallow Spanish paella pan arrived at the table. "We eat the paella right from the pan," Diego informed everyone, "starting from the perimeter toward the center. Enjoy the socarrat, which is the golden, caramelized, crusty bottom layer of the rice. There aren't many places that do paella to perfection outside of Valencia!" Saffron, the precious, earthy spice brought to Spain by the Moors, remains the traditional seasoning for the medium-grained rice. But all paellas start with a sofrito. The longer the chopped vegetables are cooked in oil, the more intensely flavored the paella will be. "I ordered their seafood paella with squid, shrimp and clams. Buen provecho!"

Traveling the Overseas Highway through the Upper, Middle, and Lower Keys was long, but road trip joy. As they crossed the graceful Seven Mile Bridge, they sang some Jimmy Buffett, including *Last Mango in Paris* and some Crosby, Stills, and Nash, including *Southern Cross*. The miles of sea and landscape seduced and inspired. They could have flown, but Diego knew what he was doing.

The Simonton Court Inn was once a cigar factory. Built in 1880, the row of cottages were the homes of the cigar factory workers. One of these historic cottages would be the Art of Seduction home when working in Key West. As they walked the shaded path beneath the palms, welcomed by the shrieking of a peacock or two, they looked at Diego in disbelief.

"This is where we are staying?" Tomas looked for verification.

"There are three pools!" Becky said, not realizing there were four.

"Maybe I'll climb one of the palms and cut some coconuts. I make a mean Headhunter!" Joshua said, getting Becky's attention.

"I thought I knew Key West, but I've never been here. The gardens are beautiful," said Jacqueline, wondering what was in a Headhunter.

They all followed Diego onto the front porch and inside their new Key West retreat. Joshua dropped his bag, grabbed a large knife and walked down the path to climb a coconut palm. Jacqueline and Diego dropped their bags and walked down the path to sit at the cigar factory foundation pool. Tomas and Becky dropped their bags and walked down Simonton Street to get some food and Headhunter ingredients.

Joshua yelled to Diego, "Here, catch! Don't drop them!" And one at a time, he tossed five green coconuts down to him.

When Tomas and Becky returned from the market they joined Jacqueline and Diego at the pool and Joshua got to work with some Captain Morgan.

Spiced and 151 mixed in a tall tumbler. Stirred with lime, lemon, orange and papaya juices, shaken with ice. Lager is slowly added. With the meat intact, the Headhunter is poured into each hacked-open coconut shell. A cherry and straw, then delivered to the poolside Art of Seduction.

"This is heaven!" Jacqueline announced after sampling the tropical elixir. "Thank you so much, Joshua."

"Holy shit this is good!" Becky concurred.

"So, all of you settle in and enjoy the day," Diego said. "I'll bring you to the club before it opens tonight to show you around. Tomas and Joshua, we need to go to the gym first, rehearse a little, and then we will all grab something to eat."

The gym's motivation had always been different for each of them. For Joshua it was football. For Tomas it was the circus trapeze. And for Diego it was the Marines. Now it was dance. Their aesthetic movements would still require endurance and strength, but now for both the art of seduction and objectification. Both required cardio, weight training, and rehearsal.

231

They all walked to the Cuban Coffee Queen on Margaret Street, a funky, little outside counter-serve and ordered five Cuban Queen Mixes. They grabbed a few benches and enjoyed the roasted Mojo pork, ham, turkey breast, cheese and bacon with mayo, mustard, lettuce, tomatoes and onions on pressed Cuban bread, washed down with some mango iced teas.

Back at the cottage, the five friends showered and dressed for a night out. A short walk from Simonton to Duval, they followed Diego past the line and into the club. Jacqueline and Becky didn't have to work yet, but Diego would be introducing the Art of Seduction at midnight. Until then, they would hang together at the bar, checking out the mixed crowd of locals and tourists. Jacqueline saw them as patrons. Becky saw them as customers. Diego, Joshua, and Tomas saw them as an audience. They all liked what they saw.

For the Art of Seduction's debut, Diego wanted to send a message to the Copa audience. Impressed with Joshua's memorable dance performance at the Ring, he asked him to help in the choreography. When Tina tells everyone they are *Simply the Best*, they believe her. Of course, the talented dancers and bartenders are better than all the rest.

After the show, Jacqueline and Becky went up to the balcony bar. This was conch space, albeit fresh water. Jacqueline knew a few regulars and they were invited to sit. She introduced Becky to everyone. Steve and Cameron, the owners of Simonton Court, were across from them. Unbeknownst to her, Becky was about to be tested. From behind the bar, "Darling, why don't you take over for me for about an hour?"

"Sure, I'd love to!" Robby opened the hinged countertop and they traded places. Becky took a minute to take inventory, surprised to see a variety of her favorite cocktail garnishes, stirrers and picks. She looked over at Jacqueline and winked confidently. "OK, what can I get everyone?"

If Becky didn't know you, she always asked "What's your name, hon?" She only had to ask once. An Old-Fashioned for Kyle, a Martinez for Jack, a daiquiri for Jan, two Margaritas for Steve and Cameron, and two Mai Tais for Jacqueline and herself. "Anyone need a beer?" She took care of the beers first and lined up the appropriate glasses on the bar.

She placed some sugar in the Old-Fashioned glass and doused it with bitters and a few drops of water. Two ounces of Kentucky straight bourbon whiskey, stirred until the sugar is dissolved. A large cube of ice, stirred again. Out of respect for the most venerable of cocktails, one simple cherry. "There you go Kyle, enjoy!"

She filled a mixing glass with ice. For the Martinez it had to be Old Tom gin, equal parts with the sweet vermouth. Add a teaspoon of maraschino liqueur and two dashes of orange bitters. She stirred until very cold, strained into a cocktail glass. Rubbed a twisted lemon peel around the rim. Finished with a stick of lemon gummy bears. "Enjoy your Martinez, Jack!"

Becky rolled a lime on the bar to burst open the segments before cutting it in half. In a cocktail shaker, she added one teaspoon of sugar and ¾ ounce lime juice and stirred until dissolved. Two ounces of light Bacardi rum and ice are added and shaken well. Poured into the chilled cocktail glass and garnished with a candied key lime gummy slice on a stick. "The perfect old-school daiquiri for you Jan. Enjoy hon!"

And finally, a tiki drink. But not just any tiki drink, Trader Vic's Mai Tai. She puts two double Old-Fashioned glasses on the bar filled with crushed ice, and rolls two limes. Into the cocktail shaker, two ounces of St. James 15-year Hors D'Age rum, two ounces Appleton Extra, the juice of the sliced limes, one ounce curacao, ½ ounce orgeat, and ½ ounce rock-candy syrup. Shaken well and poured equally into the two glasses. She carves a design into the lime shells as garnish along with a sprig of fresh mint and a palm tree swizzle stick. "And for you, Jacqueline. The best Mai Tai you'll ever have!" They raised their glasses, followed by that wonderful clink, and took a sip. "Fuck, that's good!" Becky proudly announced, to the applause of her new fresh water conch customers.

She looked around to see if anyone else needed anything and saw Steve pointing to their empty Margarita glasses. "Oh shit! I forgot about you two! Saved the best for last!" Two more limes were rolled and sliced. She ran a lime wedge around the rims of two Mexican blue rimmed glasses and dipped them in salt. Slightly embarrassed, she looked for the highest quality blanco, 100% agave. She pulled the Reserva Tequila Partida Blanco. In the shaker she combined four ounces tequila, two ounces Cointreau, and the lime juice. Filled with ice, shaken until the metal begins to frost over and strained over fresh ice. Garnished with candied lime wheels, she presents the fresh, crisp drinks. "I got you something to go with your Margaritas, gentlemen," she smiled as Tomas and Joshua crossed over the balcony seating toward them.

The Art of Seduction was performing regularly at the Copa in Key West and Ft. Lauderdale. Diego had dancers in NYC, Atlanta, and Boston. Finally, there was an opportunity in South Beach. In 1989, his friend Andrew Delaplaine took over the lease of China Club and renamed it the Warsaw Ballroom. That same year, David Padilla had been offered the resident DJ spot. Diego wanted the resident entertainment spot.

The three visionaries met for a late lunch at Joe's Stone Crab and ordered three Joe's Bar

Classics and a bottle of Napa Valley Sauvignon Blanc, paired nicely with the mustard sauce. Unlike most other crabs, the Florida Stone Crab is not killed when the one claw is harvested and the crab is sent back into the sea with the other claw intact, so it can defend itself against predators. Joe's serves the market priced claws chilled and cracked.

Dipping a claw into the mustard sauce, "I want everyone talking about Warsaw," Andrew told David and Diego, "including the Miami Beach police." Tucked away in a corner of the restaurant, surrounded by empty mid-afternoon tables, a business plan of music and alcohol and sex would become legendary.

Diego and Jacqueline walked into the gutted, open space. The grand re-opening was giving the hammering and sawing a rhythmic sound of panic. The white hard hat floated on top of Jacqueline's bouffant, a unique accessory to her white pant suit. Plumbers, electricians and carpenters all gave her a second look, and smiled. "There's George," Diego pointed over to the stage.

"Hey, good to see you two!" he said, opening the drawings and spreading them out on the stage. "So this will be the new Warsaw Ballroom." Diego was impressed with the new catwalk and platforms for the dancers. Jacqueline was interested in the new dressing rooms for the drag queens. George was most proud of the new lighting and sound system. The three were looking forward to the new upper-level VIP room. Diego was already thinking about the Anniversary Party and how he would push the envelope, test the limits, and see how far he could go. He would go talk to Naomi.

She was on a constant quest to find the best erotic art in the world. If anyone could push the envelope, it was Naomi. They met at her warehouse in the Miami Design District. "Hello, dear! It's so good to see you," she said and gave him a hug.

"It's great to see you, too. I never see you around, Naomi. Traveling a lot?"

"Oh yes. Wait 'til you see some of my newfound items," she said with a smirk. "So, you are looking for the Warsaw Anniversary?"

"I am. I want people to be talking about that night for a long time."

"Let's take a walk around." From Japan there were bound prints of sexual scenes that are rumored to have served as instructional material for newlywed nobility from the 17th to 19th centuries. From the Mediterranean, there were fertility amulets and figurines. They looked at a revolving 25-pound Brazilian geode that occurred naturally in the unmistakable shape of a circumcised penis. A hand-carved wooden carousel horse from late 19th century Germany felt out of place until Diego saw its massive erection. There was the penis sculpture-slash-murder weapon from *A Clockwork Orange*. And then Diego saw what he was looking for, a gigantic gold-colored fiberglass penis that you could sit or stand on.

"This is it!" he said. They both laughed.

"Oh yes! They will love that on South Beach," Naomi said. "You take good care of it."

Diego got to Warsaw before the others. He stood in the middle of the dance floor, alone with his imagination, directing and choreographing the Party in his mind. With Naomi's penis safely backstage, he envisioned sensory, dreamlike waves that would overtake each partygoer. Enhanced or not, he was determined to make it memorable, and that would require rehearsal. Daisy, Wanda, Connie and Kitty interrupted his musing with their animated entrance, followed by the ballet dancers. Tomas, Joshua and Nelson joined them on the dance floor for introductions. Jacqueline and Judy arrived soon after. The crucial creator of the waves, David, completed the cast. It was now time for Diego to conduct and direct.

"OK everyone, let's do this!" he said. "Girls, you're on the speakers, boys take your platforms, and ballet dancers up on the catwalk. David, can you give them some music while I bring Judy and Nelson backstage?"

"Sure boss," he thought a minute. "I'll get some Martha Walsh in the empty house."

"Perfect! Let's take a walk around the club," Diego said to Judy and Nelson. "There is something I want you two to see." They followed Diego. Judy looked down at Nelson and smiled, wondering what he had in mind for them. Once behind the curtain, they knew.

At that moment, Judy made her initial thoughts very clear. "Oh no, no, no!" as they approached the ten-foot, gigantic, gold-colored, fiberglass penis sculpture backstage.

"Have a seat Judy." Diego helped her onto the balls.

"Oh, this is very comfortable!" she laughed. Diego is relieved, as he lifts Nelson up and places him onto Judy's lap. Jacqueline pulls back the curtain and she nods to Diego, showing her full approval.

The rehearsals continued almost independently from Diego. He appreciated the professionalism of each performer and was confident they would be ready.

The line had already formed for the Warsaw Ballroom Second Anniversary Party. House lights still up, Diego stood at the bar with Jaime. They were the only two with nothing to do. "The Ballroom looks amazing," Jaime said.

"It does, doesn't it," Diego said, proudly. He could hear everyone in their dressing rooms and looked around as David began his night. The bars looked ready and Jacqueline looked stunning in her leopard print dress. "It's time, Jaime. Open the doors!"

The house lights dimmed as he gave Lucy a good-luck pat, "Happy Anniversary, everyone!" And with that announcement, Jaime let in as many people at a time that he approved, and that Jacqueline could keep up with.

Diego always loved watching a club come to life. Bartenders shaking and pouring faster and faster as conversations got louder and louder. Before it got too crowded, he would go say hi to "The Butler" of the bathroom. "How you doing, Lorenzo?" he asked, standing at the urinal.

"I'm fine, Boss. How's everything with you?"

"Great, thanks. It's going to be a busy night. Got everything you need?"

He pumped some soap into Diego's hand and turned on the water for him. "I think I'm good, Boss," readying a paper towel and a possible spritz of cologne. He sold mouthwash, condoms, tissue packs, cigarettes, aspirin, gum, mints, lollypops, even contact solution. A bit down in his luck, Lorenzo would be forever grateful to Diego for this job.

Diego tossed a five into the empty jar, "I'll see you later, my friend. You have a good night!"

"You too, Boss."

As he left the bathroom, the DJ booth was to Diego's right. He stood watching as David teased the growing crowd. It was time. He signaled to the Machine and the volume of the music suddenly intensified. Martha Walsh commands everyone to dance and the house lights go black. In total blackness, she repeats the order. Just as in rehearsal, David extends the dramatic pause in total silence and darkness, then answered in a tribal rap, to dance until exhaustion. Right on cue, the Art of Seduction dancers took their places on platforms around the floor. Diego squinted in the sudden burst of intense white light, initiating the beginning of five hours of human bonding the likes of which South Beach had never experienced.

Diego knew the Party would depend on each performance to flow flawlessly, like the movements of a symphony. David's sets are carefully composed to support the crowd's rolling ebb and flow, working them hard, followed by some time to recover.

The first movement in sonata or allegro has two musical themes. The first is loud and forceful, the tribal rap of Freedom Williams. The second is quiet and lyrical, Madonna's breathless trip hop chant. Iron and silk, yang and yin.

241

After the lively and energetic first movement, it's time to relax, the adagio. The second is slower and melodic. David would tempt the crowd with a little bit of Paul Shapiro's flute double trill. His *Whistle Song* would bring them into another state of mind.

The third is dancelike. A boisterous scherzo. An energetic joke. Diego and his dancers, dressed as sailors, would escort the drag Cher, strutting across the stage in her black stiletto heels, her fishnet black stocking and black assless onesie.

The final exuberant movement is a rondo which is repeated, usually rapidly, intensely, and joyously. David's flamenco trance mix, *Mescalito*, would push the endurance limits of the partiers, ending with the E7 arpeggio chord rolling up the piano as Judy sings Gloria Gaynor's *I Will Survive*.

So this night, Diego would seduce South Beach. He knew, from the Latin, it meant to lead astray. He knew, seen negatively, it involved temptation and enticement. He knew, seen positively, it involved an appeal to the senses, leading to joy. He knew the art of seduction.

JERRY'S FAMOUS DELI

Michael was looking forward to a pastrami sandwich and a rich, creamy slice of cheese cake. He had checked in at the newly renovated Betsy Hotel on Ocean Drive and was meeting Anthony and Carlos for lunch. Warsaw had been closed for ten years. This was his first time back since Hurricane Andrew. The bohemian was replaced by the egocentric.

After Andrew, Michael had decided that he had had enough of South Beach. Hunkered down in Carlos's apartment, while the most destructive hurricane in US history destroyed or severely damaged over 125,000 homes in Miami-Dade, he thought it was time to head back north and get a job teaching.

Although they had never talked about it, maybe it was the common interest in teaching that bonded the friendship. Anthony stayed in South Beach and got a job teaching at the public elementary school. The two old friends would have a lot to talk about.

It still looked like the Warsaw from the outside, but there was no mistaking that the inside was a deli. Michael looked around for anything remotely familiar, and then he saw them. He thought they looked the same from the outside, too. He wondered about the inside.

"Hey Michael! You're lookin' good there," Carlos was the first to hug. Then Anthony. Theirs was longer. "We thought this was about where we used to hang at the bar."

"You know, I think you're right!" Michael said, as he got his new bearing.

"And over there is where David performed his magic. The Machine filled this room with joy," Anthony said, as the memories rushed back. "David had a few strokes not too long ago," he informed Michael. "He really had a tough time controlling his diabetes."

"Diego still has a dance company, but no more go-go boys." They all laughed. "He teaches Latin ballroom and folk dancing. We still keep in touch," Michael said.

"Damn, you kept in touch with Diego, but not me?" Anthony said kiddingly, sort of.

"Well, we're here now. So what you been up to for the last fifteen years?" Michael asked, knowing that was a ridiculous question. Although he knew Anthony was teaching fifth grade, so their experiences must have mirrored each other's somewhat.

"Mostly teaching kids how to take a high stakes test," as they both nodded in agreement. "I don't know about you, but I'm just about done. Work my ass off for little money and endless changes in regulations to keep my license."

"OK, OK. You two can talk about work when I'm not here." Carlos interrupted them as the waiter arrived to take their order.

Michael ordered his pastrami sandwich, Carlos the brisket sandwich with pickles and slaw, Anthony the Reuben. This was not the old South Beach diet. They also ordered another pitcher.

"Did you hear that Nelson died?"

"Yeah, I read it in the paper," Michael said. "He was very well known in Boston during the World Series Championship. Pedro was a fellow Dominican, and being no different than most professional baseball players, he needed a good luck charm."

"I guess he was working in a circus in Chile for a while. Sad he had to return to that, especially after that role he got with Marlon Brando. What was the name of that movie?"

"The Island of Dr. Moreau," Carlos said. "Terrible movie. He was also in Rat Man." They all shook their heads and smiled.

As their beer and sandwiches arrived, Anthony asked "So how long you here for?"

"I leave next Sunday. I wanted to get in two weekends. See what I've been missing."

"Cool. I can show you my school sometime next week if you're interested. Nice we both have the same week for vacation."

"That would be great. I used to ride by that school on my bike. Never thought you'd ever be teaching there!"

"We've all settled down a bit since the Warsaw days."

"True. Oh, that reminds me! The Bear got married to a wonderful woman up in Provincetown," Michael announced. "She couldn't be happier. The last I heard, she was in an Off-Broadway show."

"Sometimes I miss Massachusetts. We have to fight so hard for equality down here."

"Ah, talk about a fighter. How's Jacqueline doing?"

"She just had her 72nd birthday party at Twist," Carolos said. "She donated a couple of first edition books for the Lambda Legal auction not long ago. They went for $60,000!"

"I remember her telling me she led the first gay pride parade on Lincoln Road in 1972, protesting a city law banning cross-dressing. The law was overturned by a federal court two weeks later," Michael said.

"Those books meant a lot to her. To donate them to Lambda now tells how important their role will be in achieving full equality under the law in every state. To Jacqueline!" They raised their glasses in gratitude. "To Jacqueline!"

They weren't done with their salutes. Mac Klein had recently died at 101, working in his Hawaiian shirt until the end. Klein, who lived through the Depression, served in the U.S. Army during World War II, and became a founding member of Mount Sinai Medical Center, always welcomed everyone into his bar. "We'll go to the Deuce for a drink before you go, Michael. To Mac!" They raised their glasses with respect. "To Mac!"

"So Carlos, what are you doing these days?" Michael asked.

"Pretty much the same thing."

Michael laughed. "You know I have no idea what that is."

"I now work for the Miami-Dade Gay and Lesbian Chamber of Commerce. I used to work for the Convention & Visitors Bureau. Sure have seen a lot of changes around here since I started with them!"

"Well, that explains why we never had to wait in any lines!"

"LGBT annual purchasing power in South Florida is over $8 billion. The Chamber membership is comprised of over six hundred business. There are over 1.2 million LGBT tourists that visit here every year."

"And we spend a lot of money," Michael said.

"Exactly. We receive over $1.7 billion in economic benefit from our gay and lesbian friends," Carlos added with a smile. "So we are constantly reminding our local politicians that we want our LGBT visitors to feel welcome and safe."

"Was that harder to do since Versace's murder?" asked Michael.

"Yeah, the Beach changed after that," Anthony said, Carlos nodded in agreement.

"I remember Mac used to call the Deuce the Shangri-La of Miami Beach. He'd say that someone could leave here for ten years and come back and nothing would have changed," Carlos said contemplatively. "Except that now he is gone. But I remember him saying last year, 'Follow your dream and if you lose the first time, try again and again. I have no regrets for the simple reason that everything that happened to me led me to where I am, a very happy 100-year-old man.'"

Anthony thought about that and suggested, "Let's go to Twist tonight. It can be really fun there, but you'll see how different it is here now."

"I think Twist opened about a year after you went back to Boston," Carlos said. "Two levels, three dance floors, some outside space, too."

"Where is it?"

"Washington Ave, next to the 11th Street Diner."

"Oh yeah, should we meet at the Diner?"

"We could go there after Twist. How about if we meet you at The Betsy?"

"Sounds good. There's a ventanita at the café Poeti." Michael said, "Let's meet there at nine."

Michael walked to 15th and down Ocean Drive. The palms introduced the turquoise Atlantic at Lummus Park. He walked the sun drenched Beachwalk to The Betsy, and thought about all the times this "Colonial Grand Dame" had gone unnoticed. During the Art Deco revival, L. Murry Dixon's other hotels, such as the perfectly symmetrical McAlpin, got noticed. The pink and ocean pastels, and the face formed by the three windows and dividing lines, make the McAlpin one of the most photographed on the Beach.

These many years later, Michael noticed the four-column portico and The Betsy Ross lettering and matching sand window shutters. In a just completed expansion, the three storied Florida Georgian hotel has joined Jack Hohauser's adjacent Art Deco Carlton Hotel with a giant silver reflecting beach ball Orb that bridges the works of Dixon and Hohauser. In another spectacular architectural statement of connection, the pool is suspended fifty feet in the air, resting at each end of the U-shaped Carlton building.

The newly created pedestrian side-alley has a café called Poeti. Michael loved that the café has a ventanita serving cafecitos and gelato. Meeting Anthony and Carlos there would bring back memories of the Warsaw days. The roof is wrapped in a metal screen with laser-cut words called the "Poetry Rail".

As part of The Betsy's Philanthropy, Arts, Culture, and Education Program, the hotel hosts emerging authors and artists in the Writer's Room. Those in residence are asked to participate in a community event to share their work. In the lobby, Michael saw a banner with information about SWWIM poetry readings. The series Supporting Women and female-identifying Writers in Miami was having its Reading #2 on Tuesday evening. He thought he would check it out.

Michael walked down the open air corridor atop the Art Deco Wing toward his room. Inside, he opened the slider and went out on the terrace. A nice, quiet space overlooking the Atrium, this was the first time he had stayed in a hotel on the Beach. He would definitely take advantage of the amenities, beginning with the curated guest library and the rooftop swimming pool.

Michael changed into a Brazilian Cut swim boxer and looked in the mirror, and thought he could still pull it off. Before heading to the pool, he would visit the library. The collection of books in the room was eclectic. He pulled the 1946 Random House edition of *Through the Looking Glass*, and thought how unique this space was on the Beach. He remembered they used to jokingly call SoBe "the land of no libraries." He walked up the stairwell to the pool.

One floor higher than the surrounding buildings, he did a 360 to take in the unobstructed views of the ocean, the Art Deco District and the Miami skyline. A vantage point which reminded him of how he fell in and out of love with this place...the blues and pinks of sunsets and of exploding transformers.

He settled into a lounge chair on the east deck and simply looked out onto the tropical Atlantic for a while, and then opened the colorful diagonal striped hardcover. The red spine was worn and faded. The ocean breeze mellowed the musty smell, which would prevent him from sneezing.

Michael is immediately drawn in from Carroll's preface. "The chess problem...has puzzled some of my readers...but the 'check' of the White King at move 6, the capture of the Red Knight at move 7, and the final 'checkmate' of the Red King, will be found by anyone who will take the trouble to set the pieces and play the moves as directed, to be strictly in accordance with the laws of the game."

In the first chapter, Looking-Glass House, Alice is talking to her black kitten, Kitty, about what it is like to live in the looking-glass. Michael reads that everything is backwards, and the glass turns to a silvery mist. Looking out onto the Beach from the balcony, he ducks so as not to be hit by the airborne debris. The night sky randomly turns a bright blue over familiar deco buildings, but the neon is gone. He goes back inside to avoid the sheets of rain brought into the balcony by the increasing gusts. He walks down the hallway, water sloshing at his bare feet, into the high-rise apartment. The floors are dry, but the mattresses are up against the windows, obstructing the usual bay view of the city. Michael wonders where everyone is. Returning to the hallway, he is relieved to be wearing his bathing suit. The stairwell is providing a slight current. "Oh, hi Michael!" says The Bear as she floats on by with Nelson on her belly. He tries to pull open the balcony door, but it won't budge. Just as the water level reaches his mouth, he is startled by the splashing of pool water, bringing him back to consciousness.

"I hope you enjoyed your nap." Still a bit dazed, is asked, "Can I get you anything from the bar?"

"Sure, what do you recommend?" still not thinking clearly.

"I make a great Prickly Pear Margarita," the bartender said proudly.

"That sounds perfect!"

The salted blue rim glass is delivered, and one sip turns into a few gulps of the ice cold indigenous twist on the classic tequila cocktail. Michael already knows he is going to have a second, and stays up at the pool for sunset.

When he enters the revitalized alleyway, Anthony and Carlos are already standing at the Ventanita. They order the usual Café Cubanos, except at twice the price as in the Warsaw days.

Anthony looks in at the menu and sees they make crepes. "Let's get something to eat here before Twist. I could go for some crepes." Michael and Carlos agree. They ordered shrimp with asparagus, chicken divan, and a ratatouille and sat at a table outside Poeti.

"So how was your afternoon?" Anthony asked.

"Wonderful. I hung out at the pool drinking Margaritas and started reading *Through the Looking-Glass.*"

"And what Alice found there. That was one of my favorite books as a kid. I think I still remember every word," said Carlos.

"Oh good! Maybe you can explain it to me."

"Well, my interpretation at the time was through the lens of a boy on the spectrum, with a twisted sense of reality, but I love talking about Alice's adventures."

Michael and Anthony looked at Carlos with that teacher curiosity, and empathy. And then he surprised them.

"By the way, I have tickets to *The Curious Incident of the Dog in the Night-Time*," Carlos said. "The National Theatre in London is broadcasting live to cinemas worldwide on Thursday and the Colony Theatre on Lincoln Road is participating. Would you guys like to go?"

"That's Mark Haddon's book. I've heard a lot about the play. I would love to see it," Michael said.

"Me too, and I haven't been in the restored Art Deco building yet. Nice that we finally have a state-of-the-art facility here on the Beach," Anthony added. "And it looks amazing at night-time."

They walked Ocean Drive to 11th Street to Washington Ave, past the 11th Street Diner. They follow Carlos into Twist, with its seven bars and three dance floors, to a beautiful, lamp-lit mahogany bar with an antique copper ceiling. The faux, flameless candles gave the room a fire-code warmth. The colors of the room were the colors of the bourbons, from burnt umber to treacle. The smells of the room were the smells of the bourbons, of oak and esters.

Anthony and Carlos brought Michael to this bar for the whiskey, and a surprise. It was stocked with some of the best in the world, and who better to serve it? "Well, well, how you been hon?" Becky reached over and gave Michael a kiss on the cheek, and put down three cocktail napkins which fused with the mahogany.

"Damn, it's good to see you!" Michael said sincerely. "I've been great, thanks. So you're still at it?"

"Shit yeah! I can't think of anything else I'd rather do, especially here at Twist." She looks at the selection, "So you still Crown Royal?"

Not surprised she remembered, Michael looks at the other two. "I enjoy a good Kentucky straight bourbon these days, and don't mind if it burns a little, but I broke through the Wall a long time ago." Anthony and Carlos agreed.

"Good to hear you've graduated from the blends. I have something I think you boys will enjoy." She pulled a bottle to show them. "This is from the Buffalo Trace's Antique Collection. It's the William Larue Weller wheated." She put out three crystal, tapered mouth, wide bowl, solid base whiskey glasses.

"One more Becky. You're having a drink with us," Michael insisted. She smiles. Each bowl fills with a dark bronze pour. They each raise their glasses and wave them in front of their noses. Michael gets a little of his grandfather's pipe tobacco, sitting in his leather chair as a kid. "To old friends!" After the clinking of crystal, they take a small amount into their mouths and chew the whiskey. Becky has put a small glass of mineral water and a spoon in front of them. They follow her lead by putting just a few drops of water in their glasses and over time the whiskey evolves. Honey, figs and dates, and a lingering warmth.

"So how often do you get to Portland?" Michael asks Anthony.

"Holidays and a few weeks every summer. One of the perks of teaching." Michael nods. "The Old Port is still one of my favorite places. That seaside town and working waterfront that the tourists love. That ocean my family lives and dies working. The fishing industry is a hard life. They work hard and play hard, that's for sure."

"I'll never forget the pirate parties and clam bakes on Richmond Island," Michael said. "Yeah, your family sure does know how to party!"

"I didn't know you came from a family of fishermen," Becky reaches for another bottle. "I have something very special in their honor." She put four new crystal glasses on the bar. "This is Jefferson's Ocean: Aged at Sea bourbon." She shows the bottle to Anthony. "A typical barrel stops in five continents and crosses the equator four times on the ship. This is cask strength, so this time I'm going to add a single ice cube to each glass, after our first sips." The nose is a soft salt and light smoke. "To the Portland fishermen and women, past and present."

"Thank you Becky," Anthony says, to the sound of crystal clinking, again.

"Imagine the extreme elements, the barometric pressure and temperature changes, the salt air, and the rocking of the ship as the bourbon ages. Cask strength isn't diluted, so I hope you taste just a hint of the sea," Becky says in a hypnotic suggestion.

"A scent of vanilla now tastes like a little molasses and cinnamon," Michael observes, and takes another sip. "Kinda reminds me of cooking with my mom, except for the 112 proof burn," he laughs.

"And the taste of oak and rye is the reality," Carlos says, as the others chewed and thought about what he just said.

Michael might have been leaving South Beach when this bourbon began its new, charred oak barrel, Kentucky maturation. These many years later, here they are, appreciating the complexity and understanding the necessity of the voyage. During the Warsaw years, they weren't mature enough to appreciate and understand a lot of things.

In the basement of the Betsy is B Bar. The dark, contemporary décor has a comfortable Lower East Side atmosphere, perfect for a small community event such as the SWWIM series. Michael looked around. There weren't many men in the room, but as an elementary school teacher, he was used to that. The merlot sofas that framed the room looked very inviting, but a barstool is always a better option going solo. And then, looking over at the bar, he saw that familiar blond bouffant.

"Michael, my dear, it has been a long time!" He gave Jacqueline a kiss on both cheeks, and she stood with her arms outstretched. "Give me a hug."

"I'm so glad to see you. I was wondering if I was going to run into you at Twist last night."

"Honey, that's past our bedtime."

Michael wasn't sure if she was joking. "Yeah, I know what you mean. This will be an earlier night for sure. We were drinking whiskey with Becky last night!"

"Oh yes, she knows her whiskeys." Michael helped Jacqueline onto the corner barstool and sat next to her. "And this handsome gentleman knows his wines," greeting the bartender, she introduced Michael to Noah.

"Nice to meet you Michael. I have a very special White Burgundy I think you will like, Jacqueline. Do you like Chardonnay, Michael?"

"I do."

"Great, I'll get a bottle."

Jacqueline took advantage of his trip to the wine cellar. "Noah is the hotel's sommelier, and he just returned from Paris and Burgundy. He is also very involved in the PACE Program, so he will be introducing the author in residence. Oh, and by the way, he's single," always the matchmaker.

Noah returned and presented the bottle. "This is a 2010 Meursault Perrieres from Francois Mikulski. The 20-acre estate is in the southern commune of Cote de Beaune, a region of Burgundy." He places two delicate stems on the bar and takes out his sommelier knife. He scores below the lip and removes the foil, putting it in his pocket. He gives the corkscrew a little push and a twist, and stops when there is just one turn left. He pulls the first lever up and then the second from the lip and unscrews the corkscrew and puts it in his pocket. He wriggles the cork out of the bottle and places it on the table. Jacqueline and Michael leave it there, but Noah sees a teachable moment and picks it up. "This is what I do with the cork. I look for the vineyard's label and then make sure it is wet on the side that was inside the bottle and dry on the other side." He passes the cork to them so they can inspect it. "It feels OK, right?" They nod. "If the bottle is stored upright, the cork can dry and fail. If the top of the cork is wet, there might be a hole. Air might have been let in, ruining the wine." He then pours a small taste for Jacqueline. She looks at the color, smells it, and tastes it, and approves.

"Noah, please have a glass with us," Jacqueline says.

"Oh, I'd love to, thank you," and places a third glass on the bar. "These glasses are perfect for White Burgundy. They are hand-made Riedel Sommeliers." He pours about half a glass each. The color is a light yellow, and they all take a sip.

"Oh my god, that's delicious!" Jacqueline says. "A peachy nose which I love, with a nice balance of acidity and citrus taste."

"I get an apple and lemony aroma, and that buttery, intense flavor of the Chardonnay," adds Michael. "For me, this is a perfect wine to drink without food."

"I agree, Michael. I first tasted this wine at the domaine and it has become one of my favorites. It has great spice and lots of weight, complexity and length." From the looks on their faces, he saw another teachable moment.

"This Perrieres is 13.2%, and weight relates to the presence of alcohol and the degree of body in a wine, light, medium, or full. Swirl the wine in your glasses and observe how wide the tears are on the side of the glass and how quickly they move down the glass." He waits, then continues. "The tears of this wine are fairly slow to move, so the wine is a higher alcohol content and full-bodied.

The length of a wine simply relates to the amount of time the taste and aroma linger after swallowing. The longer the better.

The complexity of a wine is the combination of richness, balance, and flavor intensity. All great wines have an element of complexity. With a little more time, this wine could gain even more complexity."

"Well, I certainly have learned a lot about whiskey and wine this week," Michael said. "Thanks for sharing some of your knowledge with us, Noah."

"You're welcome," he checked his watch. "I'll be back after I open the program and make the introductions. Enjoy!" Michael thought about the time he met Diego, and smiled at Jacqueline.

"Good evening everyone and welcome to B Bar at the Betsy South Beach. As part of our Philanthropy, Arts, Culture, and Education Program, the hotel hosts emerging authors and artists in the Writer's Room. This is our second reading of the series with Supporting Women and female-identifying Writers in Miami. Please welcome our resident author and musician, Judy Gerard!"

As Judy entered the room to enthusiastic applause, and sat in one of two goldenrod Queen Anne chairs to either side of the microphone, Michael turns to Jacqueline, "Holy shit, it's The Bear!"

"Dear, she hasn't gone by The Bear in many years. But those Provincetown and Key West years are very special to her."

"Such good memories." Michael poured them some more wine, and remembered a few. "So you have stayed in touch with her?"

"Oh yes, we are very good friends. I am here to support her tonight. You'll hear why."

"When we received and read Judy's application to the Writer's Room residency, some of us already knew who she was and what she had accomplished," Noah began his introduction. "Some of you may have waited in line to hear her sing at the Pied in Provincetown or at La Te Da in Key West." The audience applauded. "And then there was the Anniversary Party at Warsaw here on the Beach." Michael and Jacqueline applauded the loudest and longest. "Broadway and two successful albums later, she is with us tonight to share a work she needed to finish. So it is with great honor, I welcome Judy to the B Bar Betsy South Beach."

"Thank you Noah, and the staff here at the Betsy, for making my stay magical. That magic began when I read the dedication plaque to the Writer's Room. 'Out of my life I fashioned a fistful of words, when I opened my hand, they flew away' by Hyam Plutzik, Jonathan's dad. I hope this fistful of words will be as cathartic for you as they were for us. We came here so they would fly away. And to Alice and her adventures, this is called *Who Am I*."

Who am I?
I am a woman. A musician. A piano player. The Bear.
I see the way people look at me.
I am a reader. A writer. I am big. I am beautiful.
I see the way people look at me.
I am a lesbian. A wife. A torch singer. A foodie.
I see the way people look at me, now.

Who am I not?
I am not a fool. Or a Republican. And I vote.
I see the way people look at me.
I am not a victim. Or a sucker. And I fight.
I see the way people look at me.

I am not a zealot. Or a faddist. And I advocate.
I see the way people look at me, now.

Don't stop. Why me?
Because you are a girl. Alone. Desirable. Vulnerable.
Don't stop. Why me?
Because you are a temptress. Pretty. Needy. Playful.
Don't stop. Why me?
Because you are a virgin. Unkissed. Unknown.
Don't stop. Why me?
Because you are unloved. Unwanted. Abused.

Stop! Why not me?
Because you are not a child. You are independent.
Stop! Why not me?
Because you are not powerless. You are supported.
Stop! Why not me?
Because you are not isolated. You are a performer.
Stop! Why not me?
Because you are not unloved. You are cherished.

Who am I?
I am a woman. A wife. A mother. A lesbian.
I see the way people look at me.
I am in love. With my wife. My daughter. Myself.
I see the way people look at me.
I am in control. Sometimes. And that's enough.
I see the way people look at me, now.

Jacqueline stood with the room, and to its background applause, walked over to Judy and hugged her for the duration. "You did it," she whispered in her ear. And for that moment, it was just the two of them, and Alice.

"That was my fistful of words," Judy told their audience. "Many of you know our Beach treasure, Jacqueline. Over the years, she has given me the courage to fly in so many ways. And now, another fistful of words." She handed the microphone to Jacqueline. "You're next my friend."

"Thank you, Judy. Hello everyone. Before I open my fist full of words and they fly away, I would like to highly recommend this cathartic experience to you all. Start with asking yourself 'Who am I?' and perhaps just as powerful, then ask yourself 'Who am I not?' and see where it takes you. So, I asked myself, Who am I?"

Who am I?
I am female-identifying. I am Jacqueline. I am Jack.
I see the way people look at me.
I am a performer. I am fashionable. I am beautiful.
I see the way people look at me.
I am LGBTQ. A devoted partner. A foodie.
I see the way people look at me, now.

Who am I not?
I am not a fool. Or a Republican. And I vote.

I see the way people look at me.
I am not a victim. Or a sucker. And I fight.
I see the way people look at me.
I am not a zealot. Or a faddist. And I advocate.
I see the way people look at me, now.

Don't stop. Why me?
Because you are a boy. Alone. Desirable.
Vulnerable.
Don't stop. Why me?
Because you are needy. Playful.
Don't stop. Why me?
Because you are a virgin. Unkissed. Unknown.
Don't stop. Why me?
Because you are unloved. Unwanted. Bullied.

Stop! Why not me?
Because you are not a child. You are independent.
Stop! Why not me?
Because you are not powerless. You are supported.
Stop! Why not me?
Because you are not isolated. You are a performer.
Stop! Why not me?
Because you are not unloved. You are cherished.

Who am I?
I am a drag queen.
I see the way people look at me.
I am in love. With my partner. Myself.
I see the way people look at me.

I am in control. Sometimes. And that's enough.
I see the way people look at me, now.

Judy stood with the room, then hugged her friend for the duration. "You did it," she whispered in her ear. And for that moment, it was just the two of them, and Alice.

The next morning, Michael met Anthony at his Miami Beach elementary school. On the way to his classroom, he was introduced to a few teachers working in their classrooms during vacation. Michael knew a few of his colleagues would be working, too. Inside the 5th grade classroom were the familiar library books, bulletin board displays with student work, manipulatives in storage bins, and desks arranged in groups.

"I remember in high school wanting to be a teacher, but I knew that diploma wasn't enough," Anthony said.

"We really did want to make a small difference, and were so ignorantly idealistic."

"If we knew then what we know now."

"Yeah, had to get accepted to an accredited college with a teacher certification program," Michael said. "But that wasn't enough. I was a double major and had to do a pre-practicum and then student teach."

"And of course, had to pass the state teacher exams before receiving our bachelor's degree. But that wasn't enough."

"Receiving licensure and certifications before sending out the resumes and going on interviews certainly helped, but wasn't enough," Michael said. "But it helped being a guy."

"True. I'm the only male teacher in this building," Anthony said. "The process now includes criminal record checks and finger printing, but it's not enough. Did you ever go for the National Board?"

"I did. Hours and hours of work. Was very proud of myself for that accomplishment. Turned out, that wasn't enough either."

"Yeah. The professional portfolios for the Board, and for a Master of Arts in Teaching, and now for our recertification isn't enough."

"Setting annual goals through a professional development plan and showing evidence of achievement and improvement in student state assessments won't be enough."

"And the staff meetings, curriculum meetings, parent meetings, content course work, and lesson planning to the standards won't be enough either," Anthony said.

"An increase in my salary won't be enough because most of it will just go back into classroom supplies and books," looking around his room.

"Our kids come to us angry, depressed, confused, distracted, bullied, and often hungry. All the classroom management, social and emotional skill development, and parental involvement won't be enough," Michael said. "The large class sizes are so destructive."

"So, what do you see yourself doing about it?"

"Retiring as soon as I can, because it will never be enough," Michael laughed with anticipation. "You?"

"Well, I've wanted to do this since high school, but maybe I'll become a real estate broker," he thought about the building boom happening all over Miami. "Let's grab some lunch at the 11th Street Diner."

Built in 1948 by the Paramount Dining Car Company, this Art Deco diner was transported from Wilkes Barre, Pennsylvania to the historic Art Deco District, and after many months of restoration, opened in 1992. Anthony knew how much his old friend loved diners. They sat at one of the red and white booths and ordered two spiked milk shakes and a couple of burgers. "Do you remember my thirtieth birthday party at Flash in the Pan?" Michael asked.

"I sure do. That was an amazing night!"

"One of the best nights of my life," Michael said. "Did you know that Patrick died of AIDS?"

"No, really?"

"Yeah, after he died, a Spanish restaurant developer purchased the diner and shipped it to Madrid."

The two friends, separated by circumstances without explanation, while devouring the burgers, wondered who was going to say it first.

"You know, I missed you."

"I'm sorry. I missed you, too."

Michael met Anthony and Carlos at an outside table at Segafredo L'Originale, which is next to the Colony Theatre on Lincoln Road. "The drinks here are great," Anthony said. "And we already ordered some bruschetta."

"This is a perfect place for some people watching, too," added Carlos.

"Lincoln Road has changed a lot since I lived here, that's for sure," Michael said. "It's nice they got this fountain working again."

"The City asked Carlos Alves to do the art intervention. You might remember his studio was over there," Carlos pointed across from the fountain. "The fish and corals are hand-made. The background tiles resemble moving water and it took eight artists to install all the tiles." He paused a while. "I sometimes come here at night just to stare at and listen to the water."

"I could see myself doing that. There is something very calming about the sound of water," said Michael.

"It's also something Christopher would do from *The Curious Incident*," Carlos looked over at the theater. "I read the book a few years ago and there were times I wondered how Mark Haddon got into my teenage mind."

"One of my favorite books. Carlos, were you ever diagnosed on the spectrum?" Michael curiously asked. Anthony looked surprised by the question.

"I was. I'm sure you two, over the years, have had to deal with a few students like me in your classrooms."

"With full inclusion, never a dull moment that's for sure," Anthony said, Michael agreed.

"I had a tough time in elementary and middle school. It seemed that people were always forcing me to do things, when all I wanted was to be left alone. Except for my mom. At least that's what I remember."

"What about high school?" Anthony asked, still confounded by his friend's revelation.

"I had an Algebra teacher that made those years easier, Mr. Hughes. I will be forever grateful to that man. He used my love of math and chess to open my world and prepare me for Boston. He was my muse."

"Mr. Brennan was my first male teacher. It wasn't until the eighth grade that I truly enjoyed school, thanks to him," Michael smiled. "He used to always talk about taking the road less traveled by."

"Mr. Preston was my sophomore History teacher. There was never a dull moment in his class! That's when I knew I wanted to be a teacher," Anthony said.

"We all took the long roads less traveled by, but we got there," Michael said proudly.

"But Carlos, I have to say, I've never seen you display any spectrum disorder behaviors. I think we can both say we are surprised." Anthony agreed.

"Well, maturity and experiencing life helped for me. Great counseling and mentoring and the occasional hit of ecstasy helped, too. We know that XTC releases a flood of serotonin and dopamine while increasing blood levels of the hormones oxytocin and prolactin. This lessens fear and defensiveness and increases empathy and the desire to connect with others," Carlos said. "There was a landmark study in the journal Biological Psychiatry that found that ecstasy produced friendliness, playfulness and loving feelings, the effects of X also increased empathy and enhanced communication, which are the abilities that autism tends to degrade."

They knew some of the history of MDMA, but Carlos freakishly knew names and dates, and continued to share that knowledge...A few people can still get their hands on the same kind of legal MDMA that took the country by storm thirty years ago. Rick Doblin first encountered MDMA in 1982 at the Esalen Institute. He formed a nonprofit, the Multidisciplinary Association for Psychedelic Studies, that conducted research intended to prepare for the inevitable illegalization of the drug. Part of that included sending letters and samples of MDMA to rabbis, Zen Buddhists and Benedictine monks. In the summer of 1984, Doblin conducted his first clinical trials of MDMA, keeping the results secret while quietly building a network of advocates.

"Are you saying that ecstasy cured your autism?" Michael asked.

"Not at all. I was always very high functioning. If anything, my mom had more to do with teaching me coping strategies and how to love."

Carlos saw people heading into the theatre. "Talking about a road less traveled by, it's time for us to watch Christopher's journey." And one more time, they didn't have to wait in line.

From Lincoln Road they walked down Washington Ave to see Becky again. There were few landmarks remaining that gave Michael any bearing to where he was. "Before we go into Twist, we have something to show you," Carlos said.

They stopped at the corner of 12th and Michael looked up at the yellow neon backlit letters, WORLD EROTIC ART MUSEUM. He was surprised that a museum would be open this late, as they paid the twenty-dollar admission. The Naomi Wilzig Collection includes over four thousand works of international art, ranging from 300 BCE to the immediate present.

WEAM's mission is to familiarize the general public with erotic art. WEAM's other prime objective is to collect, preserve and present works of erotic art of the highest quality from diverse cultures, to engage and educate the community, and to contribute to cultural knowledge of erotic art in history.

They marveled at the works by Rembrandt, Picasso, Dali, and Mapplethorpe, but it was the many insignificant works that Naomi Wilzig gathered from around the world that most got their attention. And then, in a room all its own, set in front of a blue curtain, was a huge, gold-colored, fiberglass penis. Anthony and Carlos looked at Michael, and waited for it.

"No! Is that what I think it is?" Michael said, shocked. Then amused. Finally, contemplative.

"The museum claims it's the most photographed penis in the world," Carlos said, matter-of-factly.

At 11th and Washington, they entered Twist and returned to the mahogany bar with its antique copper ceiling, flameless candles, and the smell of bourbon. "Good to see you again, guys," greeted Becky, as she put out the napkins and some dark chocolate-covered espresso beans. "Three Jeffersons?"

"Sounds perfect," Anthony said as the others nodded.

"Did you know Manny Lehman is spinning tonight?" she asked. "Manny does major circuit parties in Tel Aviv, London, Ibiza, Paris, Rio, Mexico City, Tokyo, Thailand, Amsterdam, Sao Paulo, Cologne, and Nice."

Impressed, "Looks like we will be closing this place tonight!" Carlos said. "He's worked Avalon, Twilo and Roxy in New York."

"I was at Crowbar one of the nights he was here a few months ago," added Anthony. "He did a twenty minute mix of Alison Jiear's *I Just Wanna Dance* that was wild!"

"Oh, I saw that musical in New York a few years ago at Carnegie Hall. I loved the character Shawntel. A bit overweight, she sings about her dream of becoming a stripper and pole dancer," Carlos said.

"Becky, do you know how to make a Sazerac?" Anthony asked. Looking insulted, she placed four Old-Fashioned glasses on the bar. "One more," he smiled.

"Sure, why not," as she looked for the absinthe. In one of the glasses she muddled a sugar cube with a few drops of water and three dashes of Peychaud's Bitters. Then added several small ice cubes, and from the Buffalo Trace Distillery, some 18-year-old Sazerac Rye whiskey. Into the other chilled glasses she rolled around a few drops of Nouvelle-Orleans absinthe. Stirred well, she strained into the glass and repeated the muddling, pouring, stirring and straining. Finally, garnished with twists of lemon, "I haven't made Sazeracs in a while. Tell me what you think."

Taking a sip, "That is a serious cocktail," Carlos said.

"Well done, Becky!" Anthony and Michael approved.

After another Sazerac, they hear Manny inviting everyone with his remix to *Meet Me on the Dance Floor*. "Get your asses up there, boys!" Becky demanded. "I'll hold your shirts."

"We'll see you at last call," Michael said.

They race up the stairs, shirtless and ecstatic and blitzed. On the dance floor, hands in the air, under the laser fan as if nothing had changed. Sometimes things are better left unsaid. As long as they know how to love, they will survive. And just as in Shawntel's pole-dancing dream, sometimes Michael just wanted to do some laughing, some living. He was tired of all the crying and had enough of all the dying. He just wanted to dance. He just wanted to fucking dance.

Thus grew the tale of Wonderland:
Thus slowly, one by one,
Its quaint events were hammered out –
And now the tale is done,
And home we steer, a merry crew,
Beneath the setting sun.

ACKNOWLEDGEMENTS

Beverages

Café Cubano

Four scoops of sugar are placed in the brewing carafe. As the espresso flows into the carafe, the brewer stops and stirs the mix into a paste. When the brewing finishes, the espumita layer of pure adrenaline forms.

Water Moccasin

Ice was added to a mixing glass, followed by peach schnapps, Crown Royal, triple sec, and sweet and sour mix, and a good shaking.

Long Island Iced Tea

A potent equal parts gin, vodka, tequila, triple sec, sweet and sour with a splash of soda.

Headhunter

Spiced and 151 mixed in a tall tumbler. Stirred lime, lemon, orange and papaya juices shaken with ice. Lager is slowly added. With the meat intact, the Headhunter is poured into each hacked-open coconut shell, with a cherry and straw.

Becky's Cocktails

An Old-Fashioned for Kyle, a Martinez for Jack, a daiquiri for Jan, two Margaritas for Steve and Cameron, and two Mai Tais.

Capt. Tony's Pirate Punch
2 oz gin, 2 oz dark rum, 2 tsp sugar, 2 oz fresh lemon juice, 4 oz fresh lime juice, 8 oz pineapple juice, 4 oz OJ, a splash of 7up, and a dash of bitters. Garnish with orange slices and cherries, shake well and pour over ice.

Food

Puttanesca
Named after the Italian ladies of the night, tomatoes and garlic simmered with anchovies, capers, olives and red pepper flakes

Eggs Benedict
With San Daniele prosciutto, fluffy ricotta pancakes, and a soppressata frittata with broccoli rabe.

Antonia's
The antipasto with the Veneto Prosecco Superiore, linguini with littleneck clams, William Hill Chardonnay. Yellowtail snapper and the filet, rare. Louis Martini Cabernet Sauvignon

Crêpes Suzette
Caramelized butter and sugar, added orange juice and folded the crepes into the boiling sweetness. Grand Marnier is carefully poured over the crêpes and flambéed. Each served with a scoop of homemade vanilla ice cream.

Locro
Belly-warming, hearty stew of corn, beans, pork, pancetta, carrots, squash, and potatoes. Oak Cabernet Sauvignon

Paella
Socarrat, which is the golden, caramelized, crusty bottom layer of the rice. Saffron, the precious, earthy spice brought to Spain by the Moors. Sofrito, the chopped vegetables cooked in oil for an intensely flavored paella.

Cuban Coffee Queen
Margaret Street, a funky, little outside counter-serve and ordered five Cuban Queen Mixes. Roasted Mojo pork, ham, turkey breast, cheese and bacon with mayo, mustard, lettuce, tomatoes and onions on pressed Cuban bread, washed down with some mango iced teas.

The Mews
Twist on a traditional Indian dish, the vindaloo had lobster chunks in a spicy tangy curry sauce served with tomato chutney, naan, basmati rice, broccoli, heirloom carrots & fennel.

Edwige
Fried Wellfleet oysters, blackened tuna tataki with beech mushrooms, butter-poached lobster with squid ink risotto, coquille St. Jacques with gruyere and cognac, and a bottle of white Burgundy Montrachet.

Black tamales
Darker and sweeter than red because of the chocolate, raisins, prunes and almonds. Chuchitos are wrapped in dried corn husks, with a simple tomato salsa and sprinkled with a hard, salty white cheese.

Bizcocho Dominicano
This cake for a Dominican family celebration. With a meringue frosting, filling was guava.

Pepian
Served piping hot in a stone bowl, the thick, smoky chunks of meat. The stew of roasted spices, beef, vegetables and fruits was served with rice and freshly made corn tortillas

The Hungry I
Lobster bisque fra diavolo followed by the tournedos of beef. Warm quail salade with the carnard l'orange. Spicy Syrah from the Rhone Valley. Opera torte for dessert.

WILLIAM WELCH

was born and raised in the Boston area. He received both a Bachelor of Science and Master of Education from Bridgewater State University. Bill's first career was in business and IT. His second career was in elementary education, where he taught K-6 science and writing. Bill is currently a member of The Cape Cod Writers Center and a local writing group, and is now enjoying retirement on a small Cape island with his golden retriever.

williamwelchauthor.com

REVIEWS

***** *The Warsaw Ballroom was a great read. Each of the characters had amazing personalities. It had my attention throughout each chapter, reading how these characters met and developed their friendships, and how life was in the 80's in South Beach, Provincetown, Boston, and New York.* An Amazon Customer 6/28/2018

***** I can taste this tale from here. *What a great book! Definitely captures a moment in time, the (pretty much) pre-AIDS 80s, when gay life seemed it could be a never-ending party. It brings all the sights, sounds, and scents of Miami, New England, and New York to the reader. The descriptions were so vivid, I felt as if I was hanging out with these characters, enjoying a delicious meal or dancing the night away. The characters are well drawn out and three-dimensional. Their different takes on the lead-up to the fantastic second anniversary party at the Warsaw Ballroom is clever and revealing. An interesting depiction of the many facets of shared joy. These characters are not without their flaws, and we love them the more for that.*
MBM 7/2/2018

Made in the USA
Monee, IL
03 January 2021

56387558R00166